RACHEL SPINELLI PUNCHED ME IN THE FACE

RACHEL SPINELLI PUNCHED ME IN THE FACE

PAUL ACAMPORA

SQUARE
FISH

ROARING BROOK PRESS
NEW YORK

**SQUARE
FISH**

An Imprint of Macmillan

RACHEL SPINELLI PUNCHED ME IN THE FACE.
Copyright © 2011 by Paul Acampora.
All rights reserved. Printed in the United States of America by
R. R. Donnelley & Sons Company, Harrisonburg, Virginia.
For information, address
Square Fish, 175 Fifth Avenue, New York, NY 10010.

Square Fish and the Square Fish logo are trademarks of Macmillan and are used
by Roaring Brook Press under license from Macmillan.

Library of Congress Cataloging-in-Publication Data
Acampora, Paul.
  Rachel Spinelli punched me in the face / Paul Acampora.
      p.   cm.
  Summary: When fourteen-year-old Zachary and his father move to
Falls, Connecticut, he spends a summer falling in love, coming to terms
with his mother's absence, and forming eclectic friendships.
  ISBN 978-1-250-01669-0
  [1. Friendship—Fiction. 2. Moving, Household—Fiction. 3. Single-
parent families—Fiction. 4. Trumpets—Fiction. 5. Musicians—Fiction.
6. Family life—Connecticut—Fiction. 7. Connecticut—Fiction.] I. Title.

PZ7.A17298Rac 2011
[Fic]—dc22

                                                          2010027436

Originally published in the United States by Roaring Brook Press
First Square Fish Edition: February 2013
Square Fish logo designed by Filomena Tuosto
mackids.com

2 4 6 8 10 9 7 5 3 1

AR: 3.6 / LEXILE: 550L

For Nicholas & Gabrielle & especially Debbie

RACHEL SPINELLI PUNCHED ME IN THE FACE

CHAPTER 1

For several days, after Dad and I discovered that Mom had gone, we tried very hard to lie. We pretended that she would be coming back even though we both knew better. Dad said things like, "We should paint the kitchen before Mom gets home." I said, "Don't forget to pick up some tea for Mom at the grocery store."

But we couldn't keep it up for long. We never did paint the kitchen. We never did buy the tea. And one night, when Dad put a bowl of spaghetti on the table between us, I said, "Mom wouldn't like this."

Dad took a bite. "Too plain?"

I nodded.

"Your mother's a lot of things," said Dad, "but she's not plain."

Once a week, Mom tried to serve up some kind of complicated recipe made out of strange textures and exotic spices. More than half of those concoctions ended up in the trash.

"You know the difference between my cooking and your mother's?" Dad said.

"Yours tastes good?" I said.

"You got that right."

Dad spoke with a Louisiana drawl he got from growing up in New Orleans. That's where my parents first met. Dad was finishing college and paying for school by playing trumpet with six or eight different bands. Mom was on vacation and noticed my father on the stage of some club. She went to see him play every night until finally he said hello. A few months after that, Dad moved to Copper Lake, Colorado, Mom's hometown. I was born a year later in a spare bedroom at my grandfather's old ranch house.

"Did you and Mom ever think about moving back to New Orleans?" I asked Dad.

"I wouldn't have said no to New Orleans," he told me.

Dad and I ate the rest of the spaghetti without speaking. When we were done, we cleared the table and washed our things in the sink. Finally, I said, "She's not coming back, is she?"

My father hesitated for just a moment before he answered. "No, Zachary. I don't think so." We returned the pot and plates to their shelves, then we stepped outside to watch the setting sun throw strange, brown shadows across the desert. "How about we go for a ride?" asked Dad.

"Okay." I stepped into the passenger side of our old Jeep, and Dad slid behind the wheel.

"Buckle up," Dad told me.

"Don't want to get a ticket, huh?"

"The police around here don't give tickets," said Dad. "They just shoot you."

I rolled my eyes. My father was Copper Lake's lone police officer. "I don't think we'll have to worry about that."

The Jeep started, and we headed west. After a short ride, we pulled onto an old dirt access road and bounced a little farther into rough, open space. Dad shut off the engine, and the two of us stepped outside to sit on the front bumper and stare at the desert. A deep, heavy quiet settled around us. "I never really liked this view," Dad finally said.

"Did you like it when you thought the land might be yours one day?"

Before I was born, my Mom's father owned all the land around us. After he died, my parents discovered that the old man hadn't paid taxes in living memory. Rather than inheriting a thousand Colorado acres, Mom and Dad got a postage-stamp sized lot and the aluminum-sided trailer where we lived.

Dad considered my question. "Honestly," he told me, "I can't say that I did."

At night, Mom used to study maps and memos hoping to find a loophole that would require the government to return the land to our family. "Was there ever really a chance of getting it back?" I asked.

"Nope," said Dad.

I can't say I was disappointed. On one far corner of the property, an abandoned mine pond held an orangey-brown chemical slick that made rainbow patterns in the sun. I saw a duck land in the pond once. The bird gave a frantic quack, a couple flaps, and then it collapsed dead in the water. I wouldn't want to be responsible for that.

I leaned my head back and watched twinkling stars reveal themselves above us. I wish I could say that I knew all the constellations, but my attempts to memorize them always failed. To me, the stars looked like ten thousand musical notes sprinkled randomly across the sky. In the darkening light, I turned and glanced at my father's face. A tear ran down his cheek. I'd never seen him cry. I didn't know what to say or do, but then I remembered Dad's trumpet in the back seat. I grabbed the horn and pushed it toward my father. "Play something."

He shook his head. "You do it, Zachary."

I could play, but not like Dad. I pressed the trumpet into his hands. "Play," I said again.

Dad took the instrument and examined the valves and the brass bell as if he'd never seen them before. Finally, he lifted the horn to his lips, took a breath, and then started to blow.

Before I was born, my father played for big time recording stars and no name brass bands. Now, in the middle of nowhere, he made a song just for me. It soared high into the sky then deep down like a punch in the gut. It was a mad, lonely tune that sounded like coyotes in the desert and my mother sneaking away before dawn. Dad played and played then finally let the last whisper of music fade like a prayer into the desert.

We were both quiet for a long time. "That was good," I finally said.

Dad returned the trumpet to me. "I think we should get away from here," he said.

I stood. "Do you mean away from this spot or away from Copper Lake?"

"I think I mean both," said Dad.

I wasn't sure I wanted to leave Colorado, but staying didn't feel like a solution to anything either. I'd lived in Copper Lake for my whole life, but I didn't feel especially connected to the place. With school a bumpy, forty-five minute bus ride away, my group of friends was small and not particularly close. I'd certainly never had anything even vaguely resembling a girlfriend. And living in a metal box at the edge of town did not put us in the mix of whatever social life even existed in this tiny corner of the world. Now that Mom was gone, leaving felt as sensible as staying.

A few days later, my father told me about a town

in Connecticut that needed a police officer. "What do you think?" he asked.

I sat at our kitchen table. The walls around me were covered with posters that Mom left behind. They were pictures and paintings of faraway places and cruise ship destinations. Months earlier, she'd announced that it had always been her dream to work on a cruise ship. Now I held a short letter that contained Mom's cell phone number, her new e-mail address, and a short note explaining that she'd decided to get away and follow that dream.

"I think that it's not fair that Mom might be in Cancún or Bermuda or Fiji, and we're still checking our shoes for bark scorpions in the morning."

Dad nodded.

"What do you want?" I asked my father.

"I want us to be happy," he told me.

"That's all?"

"That would be enough."

I glanced around our kitchen, which looked like the break room in a travel agent's office. I recalled the arguments, some quiet and some not, between my parents during the past year. There'd been weeks when no more than a couple words passed between them and days when the orange poison pond had been a more pleasant spot than any place inside our house. I turned to my father. "Happy would be nice," I said. "Let's try it."

CHAPTER 2

DAD AND I ARRIVED IN FALLS, Connecticut, on a Saturday. We'd crossed ten states in three days, and we were both ready to get out of the Jeep. Now it was the last day of April, and we were in a place that was as green as Copper Lake was brown. We found tree-lined streets and a pretty downtown. We drove around until we found the tidy, lemon-colored house that Dad rented for us over the Internet. A key beneath the welcome mat opened the front door. Inside, we found hardwood floors, pine cabinets, and soft, scuffed furniture. Ceiling-high bookshelves held dictionaries and children's books and paperback novels all bunched together.

Dad pulled a tattered *Winnie-the-Pooh* off the bookshelf. "The Web site said fully furnished. They weren't kidding."

I ran a hand over the fireplace mantle. "Mom would like this."

"I doubt it." Dad wouldn't speak badly about

Mom, but he couldn't hide the fact that he was angry and hurting.

"Why not?" I asked.

"It's no cruise ship. There's no dolphins, no sea breezes, and no shuffleboard tournaments. What's for her to like?"

"No sharks, no tidal waves, and no seasickness," I suggested.

Dad lowered himself into a rocking chair. "We're less than an hour's ride from the ocean, Zachary. Anything's possible."

I'd never seen the ocean, and I was about to ask Dad if we could go there when the doorbell rang.

"Who could that be?" said Dad.

Both of us hesitated. We didn't know anybody in this town, and suddenly, I worried that it was my mother at the door. Dad sent her our forwarding address before we left Colorado, and it would be just like her to show up out of the blue.

"Do you want me to get it?"

"Sure." A little Louisiana faded out of Dad's voice, and a bit of police officer crept in. "I'll come too."

I crossed the small living room and swung the front door open. Instead of my mother, a slender, black-haired girl stood on the stoop. With both hands on her hips and her feet in a sort of ready-for-anything stance, she made me think of a sumo wrestler, if sumo wrestlers could be small, pretty, and female.

"Are you the new neighbor?" she asked.

"I guess so," I said.

She turned and pointed at a low-slung, red brick house. "I live across the street."

"Hi," I said.

"You must be Rachel Spinelli," said Dad.

She looked over my shoulder. "How'd you know that?"

I wondered the same thing.

"I'm going to be Falls' new police officer. It's my job to know stuff." My father held out his hand. "I'm Officer Beatrice." He nodded toward me. "This is Zachary."

Rachel shook Dad's hand. "So my reputation precedes me?"

"I'm afraid so," Dad told her.

"Excellent," said Rachel. She turned my way. "Do you know about me too?"

I shook my head. "Should I?" I couldn't help wondering if she was a murderer or a bank robber or something.

"Good question." She glanced over my shoulder and into the house. "Do you have brothers or sisters or anything?"

"It's just us," I said.

"I have a brother," said Rachel. "That's what I came here to talk to you about."

"Would you like to come in?" asked Dad.

Rachel stepped into our new living room and looked around. "This is nice."

"We've done what we can in the two minutes that we've lived here," Dad told her.

That made Rachel laugh.

"What's the story with your brother?" Dad asked.

"I watch out for him," said Rachel. "I always ask new neighbors to keep an eye on him too."

"He's a handful?" asked Dad.

"You could say that."

"Tell us what to look out for," my father said.

"Teddy has dark hair. Brown eyes. He's about six-and-a-half feet tall."

"Six and a half feet?" I said. "How old is he?"

"He just turned seventeen."

"Am I going to be writing speeding tickets at the end of my own driveway?" asked Dad.

"Teddy doesn't drive." Rachel said it as if the thought of her brother behind a steering wheel was the most ridiculous thing she'd ever heard.

"Okay," said Dad. "So if I understand what you're telling us, you've got a six-and-a-half foot, seventeen-year-old brother who doesn't have his driver's license, and he needs you and the whole neighborhood to look out for him."

"That's about right," said Rachel.

"What's wrong with him?" I asked.

"There is nothing wrong with my brother,"

Rachel shot back. "At school, some people say that he's stupid. They're the ones that are stupid. Can you just keep an eye out for him?"

"No problem," said Dad.

Rachel turned to me. "What about you?"

"Sure," I said.

"And you won't be stupid?"

"Zachary's not stupid," said Dad.

Rachel nodded. "That's good to know."

"You should bring Teddy over so that we can meet him," my father offered.

"Okay," said Rachel, "but not today."

"Why not?" I was curious about this giant mystery boy who was perfectly normal according to Rachel but needed his own personal neighborhood watch.

"I've got to go to work," said Rachel.

"You're old enough to work?" I asked.

Rachel headed toward the door. "I'm fourteen."

"Same as Zachary," said Dad.

"I work for my father," Rachel explained. "He runs the Falls Diner downtown. My parents started it before I was born."

"Does Teddy work there too?" I asked.

"Sometimes."

"And your mom?"

"My mom sits on a shelf inside an old coffee pot that we keep above the cash register."

Neither Dad nor I knew how to respond to that.

"It's her ashes. She's dead."

"Sorry to hear that," said Dad.

"Don't worry. The pot's glued and screwed shut. We can't mix her in with the decaf or anything."

"That's not what I meant," said Dad.

Rachel grinned. "I know. But there's no need to apologize. She died when I was born, which makes it more my fault than yours."

"Newborns aren't typically held responsible for that sort of thing," said Dad.

"Good point." Rachel turned and headed toward the door. Before she left, she noticed my horn case sitting on the floor. "Trumpet?" she asked.

I nodded.

"Who plays?"

"The entire household," Dad told her.

I pointed at my father. "He's better than me."

"Zachary's not bad," Dad said just before he slipped out of the room, leaving me alone with this girl who seemed like she was part tiny Wonder Woman and part big guard dog.

Rachel looked around for a moment. "Where's your mom?" she asked.

"She's not with us," I said.

"Dead like mine?"

"Just gone."

"Sorry," Rachel said.

I shrugged. "Don't apologize. It's more my fault than yours." I wanted to add something funny about how Mom was sealed tight inside a coffee pot on a cruise ship somewhere, but all that came out was a clearing my throat kind of sound.

"Hey," said Rachel, "are you going to play trumpet in the band at school?"

"I guess so," I said without thinking.

"Teddy's in the band."

"What about you?" I asked.

"The only thing I play is the radio."

"I guess I'll meet your brother at school then."

"I'll tell him to look out for you." Rachel stopped in the doorway. "Teddy could use a friend."

"A friend who's not stupid," I said.

"Not stupid is sort of a requirement." Rachel smiled, turned away, and left our house.

CHAPTER 3

I FOUND DAD IN THE KITCHEN. "How did you know that girl?"

"I used one of my superpowers," he said.

"Which one?" Dad had this thing about superpowers. He thought everybody had some. Fortunately, he only used his own superpowers for good.

"The one that lets me see into the future and recognize people who are probably going to give me a headache."

"Rachel's a headache?"

"Could be."

"How do you know?"

"I Googled all the neighbors before I rented the house." He opened and closed cabinets and drawers revealing dishes and mugs and cookware. "Not only that, I happen to know a lot of police officers who can check on that sort of thing."

"What kind of trouble does Rachel get into?"

"She gets into fights." Dad lifted a big frying pan from a bottom shelf.

"Are you going to cook up some lunch with that or is it for defending us against the neighbor girl?"

"I expect it's going to take more than a frying pan to deal with Rachel Spinelli. From what I hear, her superpower is rage. As far as cooking, we need groceries first."

"Want to check out the Falls Diner instead?"

Dad thought about it. "Not yet. Mr. Spinelli is probably busy. It would be good to meet him when he's home, and we can talk a little. I may be the cop that has to arrest his kid one day."

Dad put the pan away. "Let's finish unpacking. Then we'll hunt down some food around town."

We went back outside to unload my bike then carry in the remaining boxes and suitcases. The house had four bedrooms, a huge change from our Colorado trailer, and I claimed a neat, corner room with a bunk bed, a desk, and a window that opened onto the front yard. I decided that I'd sleep on the bottom bunk so I could hide any mess up top. Rolling onto the lower mattress, I discovered a star map taped to the bed above me. I ignored the standard list of constellations and traced my own pictures across the sky.

"You about ready for lunch?" Dad called from his room across the hall.

"I guess," I said.

"What are you in the mood for?"

"Whatever."

Dad poked his head into my bedroom. "Can I tell you something?"

He was going to tell me something no matter how I answered, so I just nodded.

"Zachary, you're a new kid in a new town. Answers like 'I guess' and 'anything' and 'whatever' are not going to help you get anyplace you want to go. Don't be all wishy-washy. Figure out what you want and say so."

"I know what I want."

"Then say so," Dad told me. "What's for lunch?"

"Ice cream."

"Ice cream?"

"We drove a gazillion miles in three days. We should have something special for lunch." I delivered this explanation with as much pretend confidence as possible.

"You're serious?" said Dad.

"I am," I lied.

Dad shrugged. "Okay, then. Ice cream for lunch it is."

It only took about a minute to drive from our house into downtown Falls. Dad parked the Jeep on Main Street, and we walked past shops and stores with names like Bittersweet Antiques, the Lion Around Bookshop, and Hero Electric Appliance Store. Back in Copper Lake, we had a strip mall with an ESSO gas station, a Mexican grocery, and a taxidermist. Things were a lot different here.

Dad stopped walking in front of a place called Coco's Cones. "How about here?"

"Perfect," I said.

"*Perfect* is lots better than *whatever*, don't you think?"

I thought about it. "I guess."

Dad whacked me on the back of the head before I could duck.

It was a sunny, warm day, and the door to the ice cream shop was propped open by a large stuffed German shepherd. Stepping through the doorway, I realized the dog wasn't some life-size plush toy. It was a real German shepherd that had been stuffed. Dad rubbed the dead dog's head. "This is nice work."

One of our friends in Copper Lake, Miss Cheyenne Kocher, was about the best taxidermist in Colorado. It was amazing the way she could bring dead things back to life.

"Even Cheyenne would be impressed by this." Dad gave the dog another pat on the head.

"*Dzien dobry!*" An old man in a green apron called to us from inside the shop. It sounded like he said, "Jane dough-bray."

A woman in a matching apron stood behind a glass refrigerator case. An older, gray haired lady and a middle-aged man in a tweed jacket sat at a round table near the door.

"Jane dough-bray to you," replied Dad.

The old man offered a huge smile. "You speak Polish!"

"No," said Dad.

"Of course you do." The old man had a noticeable accent. I assumed it was Polish. "Everybody speaks Polish at Coco's Cones."

"*Dzien dobry* means 'hello,'" offered the woman from behind the counter. She had an accent too. "Hello and welcome to Coco's Cones."

"Thank you," said Dad.

I decided to step forward and try out my new, clear-thinking, confident self in front of Dad, the world, and everyone. "I'm Zachary," I said. "This is my father, John Beatrice. He's going to be a new police officer in Falls. We just moved here, and we're having ice cream for lunch."

"Who cannot like a police officer who has ice cream for lunch?" said the old man.

"Certainly not the *błazen* who owns the ice cream shop," called the lady behind the counter.

The man with the Polish accent stood up straighter. "I am no jester."

The old lady came out from behind the counter. "You are an old fool."

Tweed jacket man stood and approached my father. "Officer Beatrice," he said. "I'm Larry Fines."

"From the library?" asked Dad.

When did Dad become acquainted with the locals? I wondered.

"How do you know each other?" I asked.

"I was on the hiring committee that interviewed your father," Mr. Fines explained.

Dad shook Mr. Fines's hand. "It's nice to meet you in person." He studied the librarian for a moment. "You look very familiar."

"I thought that the job interview was all e-mail and phone calls," I said.

"It was," said Mr. Fines.

"Then how can he look familiar?" I asked my father.

"I'm not sure," Dad admitted.

Mr. Fines turned to the woman he'd been sitting with. "This is Mrs. Robertson. She's on staff at city hall."

Mrs. Robertson didn't get up, but she offered Dad and me a friendly smile. "Honey," she said. "I *am* the staff at city hall."

I turned back to the old man who'd greeted us when we first entered Coco's Cones. "Are you Mr. Coco?"

Mrs. Robertson laughed and pointed at the stuffed German shepherd near the door. "That is Mr. Coco, dear."

"Oh," I said.

"I am Mr. Koza," said the old man. He pointed at the lady behind the ice cream case. "That is my wife, Mrs. Koza."

"How do you do?" said Dad.

I pointed at the German shepherd. "Did that used to be your dog?"

"He is still my dog," said Mr. Koza.

"Coco was the best dog in the world," said Mrs. Koza. "We could not imagine the ice cream shop without him."

"So you stuffed him?" I said.

"We loved him a lot," said Mrs. Koza.

"I cannot talk about him without crying." Mr. Koza wiped a tear from his cheek. "See, I am crying."

"Bill Murray," Dad said suddenly.

Mr. Koza blew his nose. "*Bingle*."

"What?" I said.

"The librarian," said Mr. Koza. "He is like Bill Murray's twin brother."

"What's *bingle*?"

"It is Polish for 'bingo.'"

"It is not," said Mrs. Koza.

"It is a Polish word," Mr. Koza insisted. "It means *correctamundo*."

20

"You really do look like Bill Murray," Dad said to Mr. Fines.

"I get that a lot," the librarian admitted.

"Who's Bill Murray?" I asked.

The adults groaned.

"That's like asking who is Buck Springsby," said Mr. Koza.

"Who's Buck Springsby?" I asked.

"Bruce Springsteen," said Mrs. Koza. "My husband needs me to translate a lot of his English into English."

"You know Bill Murray," said Mr. Koza. "Everybody knows Bill Murray. He is a movie star. An actor. A comedian."

"He was in *Ghostbusters*," Dad told me. "He's really funny."

"I am not so funny," said Mr. Fines.

"You are no *błazen*," agreed Mr. Koza.

"He is a librarian," said the old man's wife. "That is better than *błazen*."

Mrs. Robertson stood. "I have to get back to work," she told Dad and me. "I'm sure I will see you both around town."

"And I must return to the library," said Mr. Fines, who headed toward the exit with Mrs. Robertson. "Be sure to come in and get your library cards."

"Will do," Dad promised.

Mrs. Robertson stopped at the door to scratch behind Coco's ears. "Good dog," she said. "Stay."

"Don't worry," Mrs. Koza called after her. "Coco always stays."

"That's because he's dead," Mrs. Robertson said to me in a loud whisper.

Mr. Koza burst into tears.

Mr. Fines shook his head then followed Mrs. Robertson out of the shop.

Dad and I ordered two mint chocolate chip cones for lunch. While we ate, a steady parade of customers came and went. A few ignored Coco, but most stopped to rub his head and fuss over him. There were a lot more dead animals in Copper Lake, but I doubt that any of them ever had any visitors. "You know," I whispered to my father, "I think that Falls might be one strange little town."

"I agree." Dad popped the last bit of ice cream cone into his mouth.

"You know what else?"

"What, Zachary?"

"I think we're going to like it here."

Dad wiped his face with a napkin that had a picture of a German shepherd printed on it. "We'll see," he said. "We'll see."

CHAPTER 4

On Monday morning, Dad signed me up for the last couple months of ninth grade at Falls Regional High School. Back in Colorado, I wouldn't have started at the senior high building until tenth grade. Here, high school included freshman through seniors. In the hallways, the smallest students looked like kindergarteners and the tallest resembled combat veterans.

Getting back into the school routine was harder than I expected. It was like stepping onto a thousand-mile-an-hour treadmill. My French teacher spoke no English during the school day, and I was so far behind in science and history that my teachers placed me on a totally separate track from the rest of the class. My math teacher was tough, but fortunately I like math so I was able to catch up quickly. In the meantime, my English teacher wouldn't let anybody use the pronoun *I* or the verb *to be* in writing or in conversation. Also, he took points off for using more than three one-syllable words in a row.

"Don't worry," said Dad. "You'll catch up over the summer."

"No worries here," I said. "I'm overflowing with multisyllabic calmness. And I'm certain that summer will provide significant historic and scientific knowledge bolsterfication."

Dad gave me an odd look. "Sounds good," was all he said.

I signed up for band like I told Rachel I would, but I was only able to attend the class a couple times during my first week at school. It was scheduled for first period, and that's when I had to fill out a million forms and take assessment tests and ask the school secretary how to find my locker. I passed Rachel in the halls a few times, but I didn't see her much besides that. We didn't have any classes together, plus I'd heard that she spent most of her lunch periods at in-school detention.

On Friday at the end of that first week, I lugged home every single text and notebook, tossed them all onto the top bunk, and collapsed in my bed. I closed my eyes for just a second, but I must have fallen asleep. The next thing I knew, Dad was knocking on my door. "Hey, sleeping beauty."

"Huh?"

"There's somebody here to see you."

"Who?"

"From across the street."

"I'll be right there." I scrambled to my feet and ran a hand through my hair, which always stuck up like porcupine quills when I first woke up. I stumbled down the hallway and found Dad studying a postcard at the kitchen table. "What's that?"

"It's a note from your mother," Dad grunted. "She wrote to us from the Panama Canal."

"In Panama?"

Dad tossed the card toward me. "They don't call it the Panama Canal for nothing."

I didn't respond. Instead, I examined a picture of a huge white cruise ship against a bright, blue sky. On the reverse, a simple, handwritten note said, "Thinking about you."

My heart pounded so hard that I wondered if Dad could hear it beating. I took a deep breath, then glanced around the kitchen. "I thought you said somebody was here?"

My father, still in his police uniform, scooped the postcard off the table and tossed it in the trash. From there, he crossed the kitchen, opened the refrigerator, found a carrot, and took a bite. "Outside," he said.

I headed for the front door expecting to greet Rachel. Instead, I found a very large boy sitting on our doorstep. He wore a pair of brown, cut-off shorts, and a bright red New England Patriots jersey. When he stood up, the kid was nearly as wide and tall as the doorframe. His face was round with an eager smile. He held a trumpet in one hand and waved at me with the other. "I saw you in school," he said to me. "You're in band."

I stared at him blankly.

"I'm Teddy." He had a slight lisp, and if his words were musical notes they'd all be snare drum staccato and tuba loud.

"Hi," I said dumbly. Somehow, I had not seen Teddy at school. He should have been hard to miss, but my first week had been sort of overwhelming. "I'm Zachary."

"I know that." Teddy held up his horn. "You play trumpet too."

It wasn't a question, but I answered anyway. "I do."

"Are you good?"

I shrugged.

"I'm excellent. Do you want to hear?"

This was not the problem brother I expected from Rachel's description. If anything, he was just like his sister, ready and willing to share anything that happened to pop into his head.

"Sure," I said.

Teddy lifted his horn and tapped his foot to some rhythm that only he could hear. Then he puckered up to the mouthpiece and began to blow. Half a minute later, my father appeared in the doorway. The two of us stood stunned while Teddy played a cool, bebop version of "Singin' the Blues."

"Bix Beiderbecke," Dad said when Teddy finished.

"This is Teddy," I told my father.

"He plays like Bix Beiderbecke."

Bix was one of the jazz greats you had to know if you lived at my house.

"Bix Beiderbecke is excellent," Teddy said. "But I really want to play like Louis Armstrong."

Dad gave a little laugh. "Don't we all?"

Teddy gave my father a big pumpkin face grin.

"You're good," said Dad.

Teddy nodded. "I know."

"My dad plays," I said.

"Really?" said Teddy.

"He's awesome."

"I have good days and bad days," said Dad.

"Everybody's got good days and bad days," said Teddy.

"What do you do on your bad days?" asked Dad.

Teddy lifted his trumpet. "I play."

"What about good days?"

Teddy shrugged. "I play."

"Where's your sister?" asked Dad.

"Detention. My dad says that Rachel thinks detention is an extra-curricular activity."

That made Dad laugh. "Where is your father now?" he asked.

"Napping." Teddy's voice turned into a friendly growl. It must have been an imitation of his own dad. "I gets up early. I works hard. I sleeps great."

"Amen to that," Dad said.

"Who's working at the diner if your Dad's home and Rachel's at detention?" I said.

"Nobody," said Teddy. "We're only open for breakfast and lunch. Closed on Sundays."

"Well it's nice to meet you, Trumpet Boy." Dad offered a hand to Teddy. "You sure can blow that horn."

Teddy shook Dad's hand. "My name is not Trumpet Boy."

"Trumpet Boy's your superhero name," Dad told him.

Teddy looked uncomfortable. "I am not a superhero," he told my father.

"The way you play," said Dad, "you've got everything but the cape."

CHAPTER 5

I FINALLY RAN INTO RACHEL AT SCHOOL a few days later in the cafeteria. I was standing in line waiting for lunch when I felt a tap on my shoulder. "Teddy says your father turned him into a superhero."

I grinned. "Your brother is now known as Trumpet Boy."

Rachel raised an eyebrow.

"Talk to my dad," I said.

Before I could continue, our conversation was interrupted by a group of gorilla-sized boys who started whooping and hollering at a tall, muscular kid entering the cafeteria.

"Who's that?" I asked.

Rachel nodded at the new arrival. "Mike Kutzler. Football alpha dog. Every school needs one."

Kutzler exchanged high fives with his friends then cut around us in line, plucked an empty tray from the hands of a skinny freshman, and loaded up with pretzels, potato chips, a couple grilled cheese sandwiches, an extra large lemonade, and the last two servings of chocolate covered yellow cake. From there, he headed to the front of the line to pay for his lunch. At the cash register, however, Mike Kutzler had to wait.

Teddy stood, big as a bulldozer, fumbling around with a handful of dimes and quarters.

"Dude," Kutzler said to Teddy, "let's do this before my ice melts."

Teddy didn't say anything, but it was clear that he was getting nervous, which led to extra trouble counting out the right change.

"This dope is big enough to be a linebacker and dumb enough to be a lineman," the football player called to his friends.

I don't know what possessed me, but I yelled, "Hey! Give him a break."

The football player turned to look at me then called over to his friends. "I've got one retard in front of me and another one behind me. I'm surrounded!"

A couple of the big boys laughed, but a few more gave Rachel a nervous glance. She didn't disappoint. Still carrying her own cafeteria tray, Rachel stepped out of line and marched up to Mike Kutzler. "Excuse me."

"Rachel," said Teddy, who had finished paying for his lunch, "it's okay."

Kutzler turned to face her. "What?"

"My brother is not a retard." Rachel paused, stared at the boy for a moment, and then added, "You, however, are an idiot."

The football player's eyes narrowed. "What did you say?"

Rachel slapped the full cafeteria tray out of Kutzler's hands.

"Hey!" he cried.

Just then, the cafeteria monitor, who happened to be Mr. Behr, the Falls High School football coach, arrived. According to what I'd heard, Coach Behr started teaching at Falls when chalk in a box was the new big thing. Despite his age, his chest was as big around as a Volkswagen, and he carried himself like an Olympic wrestler. "Kutzler!" he hollered. "What's going on?"

Mike shook his head, looked down at the mess on the floor, and raised both hands. "I don't know, Coach. This girl lost her mind."

Coach Behr took a look at Rachel. Then he turned to Teddy. "Mr. Spinelli, is that true?"

Teddy just shrugged.

"I've seen your sister lose her mind." The coach spoke as if he were sharing a secret with a child. "It's not pretty, but there's usually a good reason."

"Not always," Teddy grumbled.

"She has to pay for my lunch," said Mike Kutzler.

"Make me," Rachel told him.

Kutzler grabbed the fries off Rachel's tray.

"I wouldn't do that," she told him.

He ate a fry. "I'm doing it."

Rachel looked at me and rolled her eyes. Even though I was the new kid at school, I felt compelled to offer Mike Kutzler some advice. "If I were you, I'd put those down and back away slowly."

"If I were you," he growled, "I'd spend more time in the weight room."

Rachel turned to face the giant football player. Without warning, she tipped her own lunch tray forward. A slice of pizza and an extra tall cup of ice tea poured onto Mike Kutzler's pants like a science experiment gone bad.

Kutzler jumped back. "Hey!"

Just by chance, he landed on the cafeteria tray he'd dropped a moment earlier. It shot across the floor like an air hockey puck, and suddenly, Mike was sailing backward, waving his arms like a pinwheel, and flinging fries everywhere.

"*Ooof*," he said when he hit the checkered tile floor.

"Oooooh," said all the students who'd stopped to watch the excitement.

"Now *that's* what it looks like when Spinelli loses her mind," said Coach Behr. "Are you done?" he asked her.

She pointed at Mike Kutzler, who struggled into a sitting position. "He was rude to my brother. He needs to apologize."

"Well?" Coach Behr said to the football player.

"I am not going to—"

The coach squatted down beside the boy. "I think you are." It was barely a whisper, but the coach said it with the force of a three-star general.

"Sorry," Kutzler muttered.

Coach stood. "How about we take a walk?" he said to Rachel.

"Do I have detention?"

"After school wouldn't be the same without you," said the coach.

Rachel turned to me. "Will you make sure Teddy gets home okay?"

"Sure."

Rachel flashed me a quick grin. "Thanks."

As Rachel walked away, I thought about what Dad had said about her superpower, that it was rage. But that wasn't right. It wasn't anger that made her strong. It was the way she loved her brother. She protected Teddy ferociously. That was Rachel's real superpower. Ferociousness. And for some reason, even though I'd never felt this way before, I couldn't keep myself from wondering, what would it be like to kiss this ferocious girl?

CHAPTER 6

AFTER SCHOOL, I WALKED TEDDY HOME, then got my bike and pedaled the short distance from our street to the police station downtown. I found my father leaning on a desk covered with paperwork and a couple of half-full coffee cups.

"Your principal called," Dad said when he saw me.

"For what?"

"That's what principals do when new kids get mixed up in fights."

"It wasn't a fight," I said.

Dad didn't speak.

"It was too one-sided to call it a fight."

Dad raised an eyebrow.

"Am I in trouble?"

"No," said Dad, "but your girlfriend's in the dog-house again."

"Rachel is not my girlfriend."

"That's probably a good thing."

"Why?" I noticed that Dad had a picture of him and me together tacked to the wall behind his desk.

"That is one hot-headed young lady."

"Rachel just got mad because somebody was picking on her brother," I explained.

"She gets mad like Louisiana gets hot in the summertime."

"How hot is that?" I liked to hear him talk about the place where he was born.

"The devil leaves New Orleans in August because he can't take the heat, Zachary. It seems to me that your girl might have some anger management issues."

"Rachel's okay," I told him.

Dad reached out, put a big hand on my head, and mussed my hair like I was still five years old. "You better tell her to stop trying to punch the world into shape. One of these days, the world is going to get mad and punch back."

"I'll tell her," I said. "Do you think they'll let her come to school tomorrow?"

"If I was your principal, I'd give that girl a diploma, shake her hand, and get her out of my school for good."

"We're in ninth grade," I reminded my father.

"People skip grades all the time."

"Could the school do that?"

"Declare victory and run away. It's a strategy that's worked since the beginning of time."

"I think Rachel's more of a declare victory and run you over kind of person."

Dad sighed. "I think you're probably right."

Rather than a diploma, Rachel received a week's worth of detention, but she didn't have to miss any school. That was good news for me because having a couple friends—even if one was as big as the Jolly Green Giant and the other one could get angrier than Satan—made getting used to a new school a lot easier. Just the same, school was never my favorite thing in the world, so I was happy when summer finally came into view a few weeks later.

Teddy and I got to spend most of the last day before summer vacation in the music room with our teacher, Mrs. Yee, and the other kids in band. Mrs. Yee handed out punch and cookies until the day was nearly over. About fifteen minutes before the final bell, she stepped to the top of her desk and shouted, "ATTENTION! ATTENTION!"

Mrs. Yee on top of the desk was sort of scary because she was very, very pregnant. We could try to catch her if she fell, but I don't think that would have gone well.

"I want to make an announcement," said Mrs. Yee.

Everybody stopped and turned to gape at her.

I liked Mrs. Yee a lot. During regular school days, she left the music room open for free periods and lunch time so any musician could drop in to practice or study or just hang out. Really, Mrs. Yee let us do whatever we wanted as long we acted civilly to one another and kept the noise below a dull roar. Also, if you asked politely, she'd let you put your hand on her stomach to feel the baby kick. We all took a turn because it was such a strange, amazing sensation.

"It is time," our teacher announced dramatically, "for me to reveal the name of the student who will receive this year's Mrs. Yee Award, which recognizes the top musician at Falls High School."

There was a confused buzz of conversation and excitement in the room. Pammy Zimmerman, a tall, red-haired upperclassman from the flute section lifted her hand. "What are the rules?" she asked.

"Rules for what?" said Mrs. Yee.

"For who can win the award?"

"Who won last year?" somebody called from the back of the room.

"Nobody won last year." Mrs. Yee patted her round tummy. "The baby wouldn't let me sleep last night so I got out of bed and invented this award. As far as rules, it's named after me so I make up the rules."

"What are they?" asked Pammy.

Mrs. Yee pretended to be annoyed. "Here are the rules: whoever I say is the winner, that's the winner."

"Sounds fair to me," said Pammy.

"Drumroll please," said Mrs. Yee. One of our percussionists, a blonde girl with a ponytail whose name I didn't know, was sitting at a drum kit at the back of the room. She grabbed a couple sticks and started a buzz on the snare. At a sign from Mrs. Yee, the drummer whipped off a quick rim shot, and our music teacher announced, "This year's winner is Teddy Spinelli."

There was the briefest pause while the class, an odd little family under Mrs. Yee's direction, let the announcement sink in. Then, as if we'd planned it ahead of time, everybody burst into cheers.

Nobody was surprised. Mrs. Yee joked regularly that Teddy probably played "Taps" on his first plastic toy horn and "Potato Head Blues," a famous Louis Armstrong tune, on his second. Pammy found her way to Teddy, who was standing next to me. "You deserve it," she said to Teddy. "You are awesome."

Teddy shuffled his feet. "I like to play."

Mrs. Yee stepped down from the desk and came our way. "Nice job," she said to Teddy.

"Thank you," he said.

"You know why you're so good?" she asked.

Teddy nodded. "Because I practice."

"Exactly!" Just then, our teacher put a hand on her stomach. "Whew!"

"Are you all right?" I asked.

"It was just a big kick." Mrs. Yee seemed a little out of breath.

"Maybe the baby wants to join the band," said Pammy.

"Maybe," said Mrs. Yee.

"Things are going to be so different when we see you again in the fall," Pammy said.

Mrs. Yee rubbed her back. "I hope so."

"I hope not," I said without thinking.

"Oh?" asked Mrs. Yee.

"I don't mean for you," I told her.

"I'm sure there will be some changes for all of us between now and September," said Mrs. Yee.

I thought about all the things that had changed for me over the past few months. New home. New town. No Mom. "I've had enough changes this year," I said. "It would be okay with me if the world paid attention to somebody else for a little while."

Mrs. Yee laughed. "That's not how things work, Zachary."

"How do things work?" I asked.

"They don't," said Mrs. Yee. "We work. We practice our instruments. We climb mountains. Sometimes we get to coast down again."

"Sometimes we can get another cookie," Teddy said hopefully.

"Go get another cookie," Mrs. Yee said to him, and Teddy slipped away.

Pammy laughed.

"What's so funny about another cookie?" I asked.

"I'm not laughing about the cookie," said Pammy. "I'm laughing about the coasting. I read an article about one of the *Apollo* astronauts," she continued. "He said that going to the moon was easy. All you have to do is strap yourself onto a big enough bomb and then set it off. After that, it's all coasting."

"Getting to the moon sounds a lot like becoming a parent," said Mrs. Yee. "Just take away the coasting, and it's exactly the same thing."

"Are you ready for blastoff?" I asked her.

Mrs. Yee patted her tummy. "Is anybody ever *really* ready for blastoff?"

CHAPTER 7

TEDDY BEGAN SUMMER VACATION by camping out
with his horn beneath my bedroom window. He
was waiting for me to wake up so that he could get
us started on a summer filled with trumpet practice.
To pass the time, he warmed up with some easy tunes
and finger exercises. This wouldn't have been so bad
except that Teddy arrived in my yard at 5:30 in the
morning. He started blowing at 5:31.

My father appeared in my doorway at 5:32.

"Make that boy stop," Dad ordered.

"Me?" I mumbled.

"You," said Dad.

I glanced at the clock. "Now?"

"Right now."

I rolled out of bed, dragged myself to the window, wrestled it open, and leaned out. "Teddy!"

He answered me by blowing "Call to the Post."
That's the tune they play at racetracks just before the
announcer yells, "THEY'RE OFF!"

Dah dah dah da-da-da da-da-da da-de-da daaa . . .

Teddy paused, grinned, then put his lips back to the mouthpiece.

Dah dah dah da-da-da da-da-da da-de-da . . .

He ended the thing with a big Doc Severinsen flourish, an impossible, soaring high half-elephant squeal, half-angel falsetto note that rattled the glass in my windows . . . DEEEEEEEEE!

Lights flickered awake in houses up and down our street.

"Zachary!" Dad yelled.

"I'm getting him!" I sprinted out of my bedroom, dashed through the house, and charged out the front door.

Teddy lowered his horn and smiled as I approached. "Where's your trumpet, Zachary?"

"It's under my bed." The grass, still dark and wet beneath my bare feet, gave me a shiver.

"How do you get it when you want to play in the middle of the night?"

"I don't want to play in the middle of the night."

"That's why you're not as good as me."

"You woke up the whole town to tell me this?"

"Mrs. Yee says we have to practice. I am going to help you."

I studied this giant boy on my lawn. I'd seen for myself that some people really did think that he was dumb. But Teddy wasn't dumb when it came to the trumpet.

"You could be good, Zachary. If you practice."

I thought for a second, and then said, "Okay."

"Okay, what?"

"Let's practice."

"Really?"

"Do you have a bike?" Getting as far away as possible from our house was the only way I could think to keep my father from killing us both.

"I do."

"You'll have to get it."

Teddy was excited. "Where are we going?"

I had no idea where we were going, but I knew we couldn't stay on the lawn. "Far away from here."

"What's wrong with here?"

"My father might shoot us if you blow another note before his alarm clock goes off."

"Oh." Teddy glanced quickly at the dark house. He lowered his voice to a whisper. "I'll be right back."

He returned quickly with an old, red ten-speed and his trumpet stuffed into a backpack, but by then Dad was up and in the shower so I convinced Teddy to lean his bike against the house and join me in the kitchen for a short breakfast. Just after the sun came up, Dad strolled into the kitchen and plucked a doughnut from Teddy's hand. "If I'm going to fight crime today, I will need the extra energy."

Teddy was smart enough not to complain about the doughnut.

A few minutes after Dad left for the day, Rachel knocked at the door. I led her into the kitchen where she sat down with Teddy and me. "How long have you been here?" she asked her brother.

"Since breakfast," said Teddy.

Rachel pointed at the doughnut box. "What's that?"

Teddy grinned. "Dessert."

"He also ate four bowls of corn flakes, a half gallon of milk, and a quart of orange juice," I said.

Rachel shot me an annoyed look.

"It was the only way I could keep him away from his trumpet," I explained.

Rachel was wearing faded, yellow basketball shorts and a T-shirt that said DOGZ ROOL. "Why can't he play the horn?"

"Because Zachary's father will shoot me," said Teddy.

"That's a good reason," said Rachel.

Teddy took the last doughnut from the box, stuffed it into his backpack, and pushed his chair away from the kitchen table. "Can we go?"

"Where are you taking him?" Rachel asked me.

"I have no idea," I admitted. "Do you want to come with us?"

"We're going to the park," said Teddy.

"What park?" I asked.

Teddy turned and headed out of the kitchen. "Follow Trumpet Boy," he called back over his shoulder. "And you will see!"

Outside, Teddy swung a leg over his ten-speed. I pulled my own bike out of the garage, a BMX model that Dad and I put together with parts scavenged from the unclaimed bicycles that piled up back at the Copper Lake police station.

"Zachary," said Teddy, "where's your trumpet?"

I ran back into the house, retrieved my horn, and found a backpack to stuff it in. When I got back to my bike, Rachel hopped onto the handlebars.

"You don't mind, do you?"

"What if I do?" I said.

"Then you're going to be cranky all the way there and all the way back."

"I don't mind."

I pedaled after Teddy to the end of our block. We turned left up a slight incline and then rolled down a steep hill that led into a wooded section of Falls.

"Don't go so fast!" Rachel shouted at Teddy and me.

"Okay!" Teddy yelled. But we flew down the

winding road. Birds and squirrels hopped in the branches and bushes around us, and the trees above reached across both sides of the street so that the sun hardly touched the pavement. "Follow me," Teddy called.

We leaned left onto a rough gravel path. My rear wheel skidded away for a moment, but I quickly regained control.

"Be careful!" Rachel shouted.

I glided up beside Teddy when he brought his bicycle to a stop.

"We have to walk from here," he said.

Rachel hopped to the ground and rubbed her bottom. "I get the seat on the ride home."

"The ride home is all uphill," I reminded her.

"No problem," said Rachel. "You can jog behind me and push."

Teddy started down a narrow, rocky path. I followed until we reached a rusty gate in an old chain-link fence. On the other side of the fence, a wide, brown A-shaped building looked dark and empty. "Welcome to the park," said Teddy.

I looked around the dark woods. "This is a park?"

"It's the back side of Sarah Jean Tilley Memorial Park." Rachel pointed at the building. "That's the skating pavilion. Tilley's Pond is on the other side. The place is all locked up now."

"For the summer?" I asked.

"For good," she said. "Teddy and I used to skate here when we were little, but the park has been closed for years. There's not even a pond anymore. It's just a big, empty mud pit."

"It sounds beautiful," I said.

"It's great," said Teddy. "There's a big porch on the front of the pavilion. We can sit there and practice as long and as loud as we want."

"You come here a lot?"

"Rachel brings me here when she doesn't have detention."

"When's the last time you came?" I asked.

"Last fall," Teddy said.

I laughed and pointed at a NO TRESPASSING sign hanging on the chain-link fence. "What about that?"

"That's expired," said Rachel.

"I didn't know that signs could expire."

"They can," said Rachel.

"In that case, Sarah Jean Tilley Memorial Park sounds perfect."

"It is," said Rachel. "All we have to do is hop over the fence to get in."

I lowered my backpack and examined the rusty gate. "I'm not going to hop over this."

"You have to," said Teddy. "That's how we go in."

"I don't have to," I said.

"Come on, Zachary," said Rachel. "It's not trespassing. It's a public park. We're the public."

"I'm not worried about trespassing." I reached down, lifted the latch, and swung the old gate open. "I don't have to hop over, and neither do you."

I stepped through the gate. Rachel and Teddy followed. We leaned our bikes against the back of the pavilion then pulled the gate closed behind us. It made a high-pitched squeal and then a *clank!* when the latch fell back into place.

"It's easier his way," Teddy told his sister.

"There used to be a lock there," she said.

"What kind of lock?" I asked.

"I don't know," said Rachel. "A locked lock."

I heard something rustling and looked toward the nearby woods. "I think somebody replaced the lock."

"With what?" she asked.

A low, mean growl interrupted us. I pointed toward the corner of the brown building. "With a dog."

A medium-sized mutt appeared from behind a pile of old logs stacked against the pavilion. The dog looked like it was part golden retriever, part satanic jackal, and part flying monkey from *The Wizard of Oz*.

"Here, boy!" called Teddy.

"Leave him alone," Rachel whispered at her brother.

Teddy dug a hand into his backpack and found the doughnut he'd stuffed in there earlier. "Catch!"

He tossed the doughnut, and the dog jumped so high off the ground that his paws came even with the top of my head. The mutt snapped the doughnut out of the air like an outfielder saving a home run.

"Wow," I said.

"He likes it!" said Teddy.

I took a side step toward the metal gate.

"Grrrrr . . . ," The dog's growl increased in volume and intensity.

"Don't move," Rachel said quietly.

I stopped. "Not moving."

"Here, Skipper!" Teddy called.

The dog perked up its ears.

"Skipper?" said Rachel.

"He does kind of look like a Skipper," I admitted.

"How do you know his name?" Rachel asked her brother.

"I've seen his picture."

"Where?" I asked, "On *America's Most Wanted?*" The dog turned toward me and raised its hackles all the way from the top of its head down to the tip of his tail. "I know karate," I told the dog.

"You do?" asked Rachel.

"Not really," I said under my breath. "But the dog doesn't know that."

"Nobody better karate my dog!" announced a shrill, loud voice behind us.

"Woof!" added the dog.

Teddy, Rachel, and I turned toward the sound of the voice. Suddenly, the golden jackal rushed toward us. It darted between our legs then leaped into the arms of Pammy Zimmerman, who stepped out from behind the skating cabin.

"Pammy!" yelled Teddy.

"What are you doing here?" I asked.

"Who's Pammy?" said Rachel.

Pammy brushed red hair out of her face. "I work here," she said.

"She's our friend," Teddy told Rachel.

Pammy let Skipper hop to the ground. Then she gave Teddy a big hug. She turned to Rachel and extended a hand. "I'm in the band."

Rachel took the tall girl's hand cautiously. "I'm not."

"Do you have your flute?" Teddy asked Pammy.

"I don't."

"That's too bad," said Teddy.

"Why?" said Pammy.

Teddy stood a little straighter. "Because we are here to practice."

Pammy glanced at Rachel. "I didn't know that your sister played an instrument."

"I'm here for moral support," said Rachel.

"I'll bring my flute next time," said Pammy. "Maybe I can play when I take breaks."

"Breaks from what?" I asked.

"I told you," she said. "I work here. And why exactly were you getting ready to karate my dog?"

"I was defending myself."

"He doesn't really know karate," Teddy said.

"My dog doesn't know that." Pammy gave the mutt a reassuring scratch behind the ears. "I bet you scared him."

"A scared dog is a biting dog," said Rachel.

"Teddy told me you don't have pets," said Pammy.

"We don't," said Rachel.

"Then how do you know about dogs?"

"At school, they decided that detention was not an effective strategy for changing my behavior," Rachel explained. "Zachary's dad convinced them to give me mandatory community service instead. I go to the police station a couple times a week and exercise the police dogs."

Following the incident with Mike Kutzler in the cafeteria, Dad told me that since Rachel was going to be in the dog house anyway she might as well help out with real dogs.

"Zachary's dad is a police officer," said Teddy.

"I know your father," Pammy told me. "I see him at city hall sometimes."

"Zachary's dad can shoot people," said Teddy.

51

"He doesn't shoot people," I said.

"But he could."

"You just hang out at city hall for fun?" Rachel asked Pammy.

"Pammy's dad is the mayor of Falls." Teddy said it as if he was talking about the president of the United States.

"Your dad is Jerry Zimmerman?" asked Rachel.

Pammy nodded.

"Mayor Z?"

Pammy grinned. "That's him."

"That means that Zachary's dad works for your dad," said Rachel.

"My dad works for the whole town," I clarified.

"Don't get your shorts in a knot," Rachel told me. "Your dad is my hero."

"Oh?"

"Hanging out with Bert and Ernie is lots better than sitting through detention." Bert and Ernie were Falls's police dogs.

Teddy knelt down to rub Skipper. "This dog does not bite."

"He sure looked like he was going to bite," I said.

"He does bite a little," admitted Pammy.

"How did you know his name?" Rachel asked her brother.

"Pammy brings Skipper's pictures to school," said Teddy.

"It's true," Pammy said. "I carry his picture every-where. I love my dog."

Rachel knelt down so that she'd be at the same level as the mutt. Skipper wiggled away from Teddy and took a closer look at this new girl. Rachel pretended to ignore him so the dog inched close enough to bump his nose into Rachel's leg.

"He wants you to pet him," I said.

"I know what he wants."

Rachel sounded absolutely sure of herself. In fact, she sounded so certain that it made me wonder if maybe, just maybe, she was not so certain about things as she seemed. Maybe she was like me, and she was only pretending to be the most confident person in the world.

Skipper sniffed at Rachel, jogged around her once, then approached her one more time. He stopped at her feet and sat. Finally, Rachel reached out and scratched between his shoulder blades. "It's okay if you bite a little," Rachel said to the dog.

The dog pulled his lips into what looked like a big grin.

"Everybody bites sometimes," she told him.

We followed Pammy to the front of the pavilion where I expected to see an empty pit of mostly mud, a few strips of dead grass, and maybe an old, trashy shoreline. Instead, we found several newly painted park benches facing a pond that was more than half full. Morning sun glittered off the water's surface. The grass along the shore was freshly cut, and a strip of clean, raked sand made a little beach. The pavilion's wide porch had been scraped down to clean, bare wood, and several buckets of unopened paint sat waiting for use.

"Where's the ugly park you were talking about?" I asked Rachel.

Rachel turned toward Pammy. "What happened?"

"Look!" Teddy cried. He pointed at Skipper, who was racing away from us to the far end of the pond. A couple of fat, brown geese approached the surface with wings flapping wide, heads thrust forward, and feet stretched out for a landing. Skipper splashed into the water barking and carrying on after them.

"What is he doing?" I asked.

"Goose patrol," said Pammy. Skipper barked and scolded while he paddled after the floating geese. Finally, the birds couldn't ignore him. They flapped angrily back into the sky. "Good dog!" shouted Pammy.

"Why is that good?" asked Teddy.

"Too many geese make too much goose poop," said Pammy. "Here Skipper!" she called.

The dog ignored her.

"Have you trained him?" asked Rachel.

"Not really," said Pammy. "He just figures things out."

Skipper looked up as if he knew that people were talking about him.

"He's pretty smart then," Rachel said.

Pammy laughed. "His solution to almost everything is to bark at it or pee on it."

Rachel stood on the steps leading up to the pavilion. She stared at the pond. "How did you get water back in there?"

Pammy pointed at the hill above us. "There's a little brook that's supposed to flow down into the pond. A tree fell across it so water was heading through the woods and then draining into a storm gutter at the street."

"That's why the pond turned into a mud pit?" Rachel asked.

Pammy nodded. "I got a chainsaw and cut the dead tree out of the way. Then I used the logs and built a dam to send water back into the old stream bed. The pond started filling up again the same day."

"You've got a chainsaw?" I said.

"My dad had one in the garage. He said I could do anything I wanted that would make the park look nice again. The mud wasn't nice." She leaned on her rake and studied the pond. "I think this is better."

I don't know about anybody else, but I was pretty impressed.

"Is the park going to reopen?" asked Rachel.

Pammy turned to face her. "If I do a good enough job cleaning it up."

"Can we help?" Teddy asked.

"Sure," said Pammy, "but I don't know if my dad can pay you."

"We'll volunteer," said Teddy.

Rachel shook her head. "I have to work at the diner," she told her brother. "I can't bring you here every day."

"I'll come with Zachary." Teddy said confidently. He turned to me. "We'll ride our bikes, and we'll bring our trumpets so we can practice too."

"Sure," I said.

"You don't have to," Rachel told me.

"But he can if he wants to," Teddy said hopefully.

"Teddy," Rachel began.

"It's up to Zachary," Teddy snapped at his sister.

"It's not up to Zachary to say whether or not you're allowed to come to the park every day."

"I'm the big brother," Teddy protested. "I'm older than you. I don't have to ask your permission for everything." He turned to me. "So?"

I really didn't know whether I wanted to hang out with Teddy at the park all summer, but it's not like I had better plans. "It's okay with me."

"Awesome!" said Teddy.

"I could use the help," Pammy admitted.

"We'll come every day!" Teddy told her.

"You'll have to check with my dad first," said Pammy. "I think there's a volunteer form you need to fill out."

"No problem," I said.

Teddy's eyes went wide. "We're going to talk to the mayor!"

"We'll visit him at city hall," I said.

Rachel stepped close to me and spoke just loud enough so only I could hear, "You should have asked me first."

"Why?"

"It's a little more than Teddy's used to."

"You're the one that told me he's not stupid."

"He's not."

"And he *is* the big brother."

"You still should have asked me," said Rachel.

"We'll be fine," I said.

Rachel gave me a hard look. "You promise?"

Unlike my father, I had no superpower that enabled me to see the future. On the other hand, it was clear that Rachel was not asking for some kind of easy prediction or general reassurance that things would be fine. She wanted a guarantee.

"I promise."

I admit that it was sort of a lie, but it's not like Rachel would have accepted anything less.

CHAPTER 8

The next day, I found Teddy waiting for me in the kitchen when I woke up. Rachel joined us when we stepped outside to get our bikes. She hopped on my handlebars again.

"Don't you have a bike?" I asked.

"I like having a chauffeur," she told me.

"I am not your chauffeur."

"How about copilot?"

"That's better." I pushed off and began to pedal, but I must have started too quickly because Rachel tipped back and fell against my arms. "Sorry," I said.

"It's not like I have a seat belt up here." She grabbed my wrist and regained her balance. She didn't take her hand away from my arm which made it a little more difficult to steer, but I didn't mind.

At the park, we raked leaves for a couple hours until Rachel let us know that she had to leave for work at the diner.

"I'm going to stay," said Teddy.

Rachel glanced between me and her brother.

"Take my bike," I told her. "We'll meet you at the restaurant later."

"I'm trusting you with my brother," Rachel warned me.

I used the same I'm-warning-you voice to respond. "I'm trusting you with my bike." That made Teddy and Pammy laugh.

"Behave," Rachel told Teddy, then she pedaled away.

Pammy headed to the pavilion porch and began setting out painting supplies. "Did you talk to my dad about volunteering?" she asked me.

"Not yet," I admitted.

"You have to do that," she said.

"Tomorrow," I promised.

"Can I ask you a question?" Pammy said to Teddy.

"Yes."

"What's the deal between you and your sister?"

"She watches out for me," said Teddy.

"Like a hawk on Ritalin," I said.

"She acts like she's your mother," said Pammy.

Teddy and I joined Pammy on the porch where she handed us paintbrushes and a five-gallon bucket of deep red paint.

"Rachel is not like my mom," said Teddy. "Our mother was—"

"Calmer?" I suggested.

"Nicer?" offered Pammy.

"Different," said Teddy. "Rachel would be different if—" Teddy stopped and bit his lower lip. When he continued, he said, "I miss my mom a lot, but I wouldn't want Rachel to be any other way."

"That's good," I told him.

"I think that things happen for a reason," said Pammy.

"You mean God," said Teddy.

"I guess." Pammy pried the lid off another paint bucket. This one held pine green.

"God did not take Teddy's mother just so that Rachel could grow up to be more like Rachel," I said.

"How do you know?" Pammy asked me.

"Everything does *not* happen for a reason," I told her. I thought of my parents. Mom was floating around the globe alone. The idea that my own family had exploded into pieces because of some mysterious good reason offended me.

"I didn't say it had to be a *good* reason," said Pammy.

Teddy held up a brush. "Can we paint now?"

"Good idea." Pammy pointed at the paint buckets. "The red is for the railings. I'll put green on the rest."

With Teddy and me on railings and Pammy pushing a long-handled roller across the deck, we turned the pavilion at Tilley's pond into a cozy Christmas cottage. Despite the heat and humidity—and even though Teddy was the worst painter in the world—the work was sort of relaxing. We painted the entire porch in just a few hours.

Pammy clapped her hands. "This is going to look great when we skate here this winter."

The three of us gathered at the water's edge to admire our work.

"It's good," I agreed.

"It's great," said Teddy. "What should we do next?"

"No more today," said Pammy. "We've done enough."

Teddy looked my way. "Then it's time for us to practice."

"Uh-oh," said Pammy.

"What is it?" I asked.

"I forgot to bring my flute," she confessed. "You guys practice. I'll clean up."

"Are you sure?"

"I'm getting paid to be here," said Pammy. "You're not."

Teddy led me to one of the park benches where we sat and unpacked our trumpets. Together, we did some warm-ups. From there, he showed me a few exercises to help with my slurring and my attacks and my tone. Then we took turns listening to one another play and talked about the parts that sounded good. "Wynton Marsalis says you have to hear your good parts and then love them," said Teddy.

"You know Wynton Marsalis?" I asked.

"Mrs. Yee let me watch him teach music lessons on the Internet."

"My dad played with Wynton Marsalis in New Orleans."

Teddy's eyes got wide. "No way."

"He'll tell you about it if you ask him."

"Wynton Marsalis wrote a book," Teddy said. "Rachel gave it to me for Christmas."

"What's it about?" I asked.

"I don't know," said Teddy.

"Didn't you read it?"

Teddy shook his head. "Don't tell Rachel."

"Why didn't you read the book?"

"I'm not a very good reader," Teddy said. "And why would I read a book about playing the trumpet when I could just go and play the trumpet?"

I didn't have a good answer for that.

Teddy lifted his horn. "Do you know 'Twinkle Twinkle Little Star'?"

"I think I can handle that."

"I always play 'Twinkle Twinkle' when I'm done practicing."

I'd seen this boy make his trumpet do tricks that would make snake charmers and circus dogs jealous.

Now he wanted to wrap up with the easiest tune in the world. "Why?" I said.

"Always end practice by playing a real song. You have to play a full something. That's how you get better. By doing something."

"You sound like my father," I said.

"Are you ready?" asked Teddy.

"Ready, Teddy."

Together, we started a low, slow version of "Twinkle Twinkle Little Star." Note by note, Teddy picked up the pace and the volume. By the time we reached "like a diamond in the sky," I was blowing for all I was worth. In fact, I'd never played this well. I hadn't really imagined it was possible. Trumpet was something I did because my dad pushed it toward me when I was little. I didn't dislike the horn or anything like that, but I didn't eat, sleep, and breathe music like my father. But now, with Teddy leading the way, a breeze rippling across the pond, and notes echoing off the trees around me, I couldn't help but notice that I sounded great.

As the tune neared its end, Teddy broke away from the melody and starting riffing a crazy harmony line with a Texas blues beat.

"What kind of 'Twinkle Twinkle Little Star' is this?" I asked.

Teddy lowered the horn for moment. "Follow me!"

I continued to blow "Twinkle Twinkle." Next thing I knew, Teddy added a Caribbean groove and then Pammy was skipping and singing and dancing with a rake. "Lively up yourself!" she sang. "Don't be no drag!" Her voice and our horns echoed across the pond and off the hillside around us. Teddy hopped to his feet, and I followed while Skipper barked and ran in circles. We stomped and marched and made music like we were the entertainment at a Super Bowl halftime show. Finally, I dropped my trumpet to my side and watched Teddy blow one long, last, brash note. When the last echo disappeared across the pond, the three of us collapsed onto the ground.

"Wow!" said Pammy.

"That was fun," said Teddy.

Pammy smiled at me. "I didn't know you could play like that."

"Zachary didn't know he could play like that," said Teddy.

I didn't even try to deny it. And I didn't try to wipe the grin off my face either. "What were you singing?" I asked Pammy.

"Reggae," she said. "It's what my mom and dad listen to at home."

"The mayor and the first lady like reggae?" said Teddy.

Pammy laughed. "I don't think anybody's ever called my mother the first lady before."

"What is she then?" asked Teddy.

"She's a preschool teacher." Pammy stood and retrieved her rake. "Will you guys be here tomorrow?"

"That's up to Trumpet Boy," I said.

Teddy took a deep breath and shouted across the pond so that his voice reverberated around the park. "Trumpet Boy says, WE SHALL RETURN!"

CHAPTER 9

THE GEAR SHIFT LEVERS ON TEDDY'S ten-speed made sitting on his handlebars more than a little awkward. "Can I just walk?" I asked as he pedaled away from the park and into town.

"We're almost there," Teddy promised, but by the time he leaned his bike against the front of Falls Diner, the sign on the restaurant door said CLOSED, and I felt like I'd spent the better part of a day sitting on a picket fence.

"Come on!" Teddy said. He ignored the sign and pushed his way through the door.

I limped into the diner after him. Inside, the place was small, bright, and mostly empty. A neon lit jukebox filled with black vinyl records pumped out an old rock-and-roll song from the corner. Two men sat on high stools at the front counter. One had a chef's hat balanced on his head and a white apron wrapped around a wide belly. The other man, wearing his blue and black police uniform, was my father.

"What are you doing here?" I asked my dad.

He lifted what looked like a giant bread loaf off the counter. "Eating lunch." He gestured toward the chef. "And talking to Mr. Spinelli." He pointed the loaf at me. "That's my son," he said to Mr. Spinelli.

The chef adjusted his hat. "It's Zachary, right?"

"Right," I said.

"I've heard about you."

I recalled my dad saying something similar to Rachel once. "Oh?"

"Good things," said Mr. Spinelli.

"He's a good kid." Dad took another bite of his lunch.

"Thanks," I said.

Dad shrugged. "It's true."

"What are you eating?" I asked my father.

"A grinder," he said.

"What's that?"

"You've never had a grinder?" said Teddy.

"It's like a muffuletta," Dad told me.

"A what?" asked Teddy.

"It's a kind of big sandwich in New Orleans," I explained.

"So it's just a big word for sandwich," said Teddy.

Dad lifted what was left of his lunch. "This is not just a sandwich. This is a work of art."

"Thanks," Mr. Spinelli said to my dad.

"Hey," Teddy said to me. "Are you hungry?"

"I'm starving," I admitted.

"I'll make hamburgers."

"No you won't," said Teddy's father.

"I can do it."

"You're not allowed to use the grill."

Just then, Rachel appeared behind the counter.

"Make a couple hamburgers for the boys," Mr. Spinelli told her. He turned to Teddy. "You can do the soda machine."

"But I want to cook."

Mr. Spinelli shook his head. "The grill is dangerous."

"Fine," said Teddy, but he didn't sound fine.

He and Rachel disappeared through a doorway that apparently led to the kitchen. While I waited for them to come back, I wandered around the little restaurant. Around me, the walls were covered with posters and paintings that showed carnival scenes and circus animals. A life-sized, wooden carousel horse hung from the ceiling. "Does your family like the circus?" I asked when Teddy returned.

He banged two Cokes on a corner table. "Everybody likes the circus."

He returned to the kitchen, so I took a seat and sipped my Coke. On the opposite side of the room, an old-fashioned cash register sat at the edge of the counter. A shelf above the register held a shiny, chrome coffee pot along with a couple trinkets, some photos, and what looked like a high school yearbook. I really didn't believe that Mrs. Spinelli's ashes were sitting inside the percolator, but before I could think up a good way to ask, Rachel came out of the kitchen with a platter in each hand.

"Lunch is served." She slid two plates onto the table and dropped into the seat across from me.

"Where's Teddy?" I asked.

"He's mad so he's eating lunch in the kitchen."

"Tell him to come out."

Rachel shook her head. "Teddy has a temper. It's better to let him sulk."

If the queen of ferociousness said that her brother had a temper, then I believed her. In the meantime, the smell of burgers and fries made my stomach growl, so I dug into my plate.

"I saw you checking out the shrine," Rachel said.

"The what?" I asked.

Rachel pointed toward the shelf above the cash register.

"Is your mother really in that coffee pot?"

Rachel nodded. "Yup."

"And you're okay with that?"

"I'd rather have her in the coffee pot than in the soup pot."

"What's the difference?"

"We actually make soup in the soup pot."

"What was your mother like?"

Rachel bit into her burger but continued talking anyway. "Everybody says that she was really pretty, really nice, and really smart. Personally, I think she could have been a little more considerate. Dying the day after I was born was not thoughtful at all."

I swirled a french fry around a puddle of ketchup. "She could have died the day before you were born. That would have been worse."

"Just because things could be worse doesn't mean they couldn't be better," said Rachel.

"That's a good point," I admitted.

"My mother liked the circus," Rachel continued. She gestured around the room. "She was in charge of decorations. My father's never changed it. He never will." Rachel continued eating and talking. "Just before she died, my mother called my father to her bedside. She pushed baby me into his arms. Guess what she said for her last words."

"This kid needs a new diaper?"

"Very funny."

"Don't change the decorations in the restaurant?"

"Good guess but wrong."

"Don't let Teddy use the grill?"

"That's close. Her last words to my father were, 'Take care of Teddy.' She didn't say 'take care of the baby' or 'I'm so sad that I won't see my daughter grow up' or 'I'm so happy that we have a little girl.' She said, 'Take care of Teddy.' And that's what we do around here."

We sat quietly for a moment. "And then what?" I finally asked.

"Then I spent twenty or thirty months crying in my crib and pooping in my pants."

"I mean now."

She gestured at the decorations around us. "Now, I live in a circus." She lifted a french fry and waved it in the air like a conductor's baton while she hummed a little circus song. "Da da da-da da-da dum-dum dum-dum . . ."

" 'Entry of the Gladiators,' " I said.

"What?"

"That's the name of the song you're singing."

"I didn't know it had a name."

"It's a screamer."

Rachel looked at me blankly.

"Screamers are quick tempo circus marches that rile up the crowd while the clowns and elephants march in."

"And you know this because?"

"My dad plays them for practice. He says it's easier to play a piece correctly if you know why it was written in the first place."

"I'll call him when the clowns and elephants come to town." Rachel grinned. She was just as pretty when she wasn't furious. At that moment, the diner's front door swung open, and a big, gray-haired lady swept into the restaurant. I remembered her from Coco's Cones on the first day Dad and I arrived in Falls. It was Mrs. Robertson. Only a few months had passed since we'd met. Despite that, it struck me that Falls already felt a lot more like home than Copper Lake ever had.

"Mrs. Robertson," said Dad, "I should have asked if you wanted me to bring you something back for lunch."

"Officer Beatrice," Mrs. Robertson told him, "I will be sure to call you if I get so hungry that I need a police officer to bring me a sandwich." She turned to Mr. Spinelli. "Can I get something to go?"

"For you," said Mr. Spinelli, "it's no problem."

"I thought the diner was closed," I whispered to Rachel.

"Not for Mrs. Robertson," said Rachel. "Actually," she added, "my father can't say no to anybody. Once he served a guy who came in after he'd been sprayed by a skunk."

"What happened?"

"The guy's money stunk up our cash register for a week." She took a bite of her burger. "He didn't even leave a tip."

"The guy or the skunk?"

Rachel kicked me under the table and stole one

of my fries. Just then, Teddy stepped out from the kitchen to pour himself a drink from the soda fountain.

"I know somebody your dad says no to."

Rachel glanced at her brother. "That's different."

"Really?"

"Teddy could get hurt," she told me.

"You could have been hurt when you got into that fight with Mike Kutzler."

"That jerk would never touch me."

"It was still risky."

"What's your point?"

"Sometimes dangerous things are good for you."

"People believe that," said Rachel, "until they get hurt."

I thought about all the stuff that had happened to me in the last year. It's not like I'd been stabbed or burned or punched in the face or anything, but there were days that I'd felt pretty rotten. I didn't know exactly why I hurt, but I did. A lot. "I still believe it," I said.

Rachel stared at me from across the table. "You're not normal, Zachary."

I didn't respond.

Rachel kicked me under the table again. "And I think that's a good thing."

CHAPTER 10

TEDDY STAYED MAD FOR A LOT LONGER than I expected. I didn't see him again until I found him waiting at my kitchen table the next morning. Instead of a T-shirt and shorts, however, he was wearing nice pants and a shirt with a collar, and his hair was combed like it was school picture day in the third grade.

"You're going to work at the park dressed like that?" I asked.

"We're not going to the park," Teddy informed me. "We're going to see the mayor."

Just then, Dad stepped into the kitchen. "Who's going to see the mayor?"

"Zachary and me," said Teddy.

"Oh?" said Dad.

I explained to my father about the park and Pammy and how we'd volunteered to help. Dad nodded. "If you want, you can toss your bikes into the trunk. I'll give you a ride to city hall in the police car."

"Can we turn on the siren while we ride?" I asked.

Teddy's face lit up hopefully.

"No," said Dad.

Teddy's face fell.

"But we can flash the lights," Dad said.

Teddy brightened again.

A few moments later, I was wearing my own school clothes and sitting in the back of a police cruiser while Dad steered us through downtown Falls.

"I feel like a criminal," I said.

"Isn't it great!" said Teddy.

We passed Coco's Cones, and we waved at the Falls Diner. We crossed Church Street then stopped at the corner of First and Main where a set of small, brick buildings held the police department, the library, and city hall. Dad pointed at the glass door that led into the police department on the right. "I'm going there." Then he pointed toward a set of old, wooden steps that led up to a white, wooden entryway on the left. "You're going there."

"Got it," I said.

Dad gave both of us a pat on the back then headed into the police station.

"Ready, Teddy?"

"Ready," he told me.

I headed toward the white door leading into city hall, but I only took a couple of steps before I had to stop. Teddy hadn't moved from his spot on the sidewalk. "What's wrong?" I asked.

"I'm not ready."

"Why not?"

"I'm not like you," said Teddy. "I'm not used to visiting important people."

"What important people do you think I visit?"

"I don't know. Wasn't your dad the police chief at your old town?"

"He was the only policeman in our old town," I explained.

"See," said Teddy. "He was important."

"Not the way you think. Hardly anybody lives in Copper Lake, and they're all spread out. Dad mostly drove around delivering prescription medicine to old miners. A rancher with a coyote problem was about as exciting as it got."

"Coyotes," said Teddy. "Wow!"

"Coyotes are pretty cool," I admitted. "When they yelp at night, it sounds like people shouting in some alien language."

"Do you miss your old town?" Teddy asked.

I shook my head. "It always felt like I was waiting for something to happen or for somebody to show up."

"Did you have any best friends?"

"I had friends," I said. "Not really a best friend."

"That must be who you were waiting for."

"Who?"

"Your best friend." Teddy stretched his arms out wide. "And here I am!"

I laughed. "Come on."

I led Teddy up the steps to city hall. The two of us entered like a couple of cowboys heading into a saloon. Just inside, we found a wooden counter that needed a new coat of paint. I tapped an old desk bell, and the ring seemed to echo through the whole building. "Who's there?" somebody called from a back office.

"Me!" shouted Teddy.

A woman poked her head from out of a doorway. It was Mrs. Robertson. "Who's me?"

Teddy offered Mrs. Robertson a little wave.

"Hey, you." Mrs. Robertson approached us and took a seat behind the counter. She found a half-filled cup of coffee. On the outside of the mug, it said QUEEN OF EVERYTHING. She lifted it, took a sip, and then made a face. "That is vile."

"Why do you drink it?" asked Teddy.

"Because I like it."

Teddy looked confused.

"Don't try and figure me out, honey. I confuse myself sometimes."

"I'm Teddy," said Teddy.

"I know who you are," she said.

"You do?"

She reached across the counter to shake Teddy's hand. "I'm Linda Robertson. I've lived in Falls my whole life. Your mother trick-or-treated at my door when she was a little girl, and I watched your dad play Little League baseball in the field across the street from my house. Your parents still look the same to me now as they did when they were kids."

"My mother is dead," said Teddy.

"Not to me," said Mrs. Robertson.

"This is Zachary," said Teddy.

"Zachary and I have met."

I gave her a smile. "Hi, Mrs. Robertson."

"What do you boys need in city hall?"

"We want to volunteer at Tilley's Park," Teddy told her.

"Pammy Zimmerman said we needed to get the mayor's permission," I explained.

"Pammy is the mayor's daughter," said Teddy.

"I believe I've heard of her," the Queen of Everything said.

Just then, a man entered the office. He stood behind me and Teddy and waited for his turn to speak to Mrs. Robertson.

"So can we see him?" asked Teddy.

The Queen of Everything glanced over our shoulders and nodded a greeting at the newcomer. "Does the mayor know you're coming?"

"Not really," I admitted.

"But we really want to help at the park," said Teddy.

"I don't know if the mayor has time today."

The man stepped forward. "It's okay, Linda. I'll take them back. I'm sure the mayor has five minutes to meet with a couple of constituents."

Mrs. Robertson opened a drawer and pulled out two printed sheets. She handed one to me and one to Teddy. "Fill out these volunteer forms, get the mayor's signature on the bottom, then bring them back to me."

"Thanks," I told her.

"Don't keep him long," she added. "The mayor's on a tight schedule today."

"Okay," I promised.

"Zachary," Teddy whispered loudly as we followed the man down a hallway lined with old photographs of Falls. "What's a constituent?"

"A constituent is somebody who votes," the man explained.

"We're too young to vote," Teddy told him.

"You'll be voting soon enough," he said. "At least I hope so."

We entered a large meeting room where a couple dozen folding chairs sat facing a long table. "What is this place?" asked Teddy.

"This is where we make the sausages," said the man.

"The what?"

"Famous quote about government," the man said. "There are two things nobody should have to watch being made. One is law. The other is sausages."

"Who said that?" I asked.

"It sounds like Winston Churchill, but it might have been Oscar Mayer. I forget."

We crossed the meeting room and entered a door labeled MAYOR. The office inside was crammed tight with several wooden chairs, an enormous desk, and floor-to-ceiling bookshelves that seemed to hold nothing but file folders and stacks of paper. There was no one but us inside.

"Should we be in here?" I asked.

Before the man could answer, the phone rang. He leaned across the desk, punched a button on the receiver, and said, "Yes, Linda? . . . I see . . . Got it . . . Thanks." He hung up, plopped into the black chair behind the mayor's desk, and said, "So you want to do some work at Sarah Jean Tilley Memorial Park?"

"Are you Pammy's dad?" asked Teddy.

"I am."

"You're the mayor?" I said.

The man laughed, stood, and stuck out a hand. "I'm Jerry Zimmerman."

Teddy offered a big smile and took the mayor's hand. "I'm Teddy."

The mayor shook then turned to me. "And you are?"

"Zachary Beatrice, sir."

"John Beatrice's son?"

I nodded.

Mayor Zimmerman shook my hand then sat in the chair behind the desk. "And you both know my daughter?"

"We're all in the band," said Teddy.

"Are you the same Teddy who won that award at the end of the school year?" the mayor asked.

"That's him," I said.

"Congratulations," said the mayor. "Have a seat."

"Thank you," said Teddy.

Teddy and I took a couple of chairs that faced the mayor's desk. Mr. Zimmerman was slim and fit with an easy smile and a bushy mustache. He wore wire-rimmed glasses, a wrinkled, white dress shirt, blue jeans, and a pair of old running shoes. He didn't look at all like I expected.

"You're really the mayor?" I asked.

"I'm really the mayor," said Mr. Zimmerman.

The walls around us held old photos and framed documents. A dark painting behind the mayor's desk showed a paunchy, angry-faced man in a pin-striped suit. I pointed at the portrait. "I was expecting some-one like that."

"That's Elias Falls," said Mr. Z. "He does look like a real mayor. But Mr. Falls has been dead for more than a century. You're stuck with me."

"That's okay," I said.

"So I hear you're interested in Sarah Jean Tilley."

"We're interested in her park," said Teddy.

"That's great," said the mayor.

"We want to help clean it up. It's going to be our job," Teddy told him. "We'll be Pammy's assistants."

"You understand that I can't pay you," said Mr. Zimmerman.

"We didn't come to get paid." I pushed the forms that Mrs. Robertson had given us toward the mayor. "We came to ask for permission to volunteer."

"Pammy said we had to talk to you before she could say yes," said Teddy.

The mayor smiled. "So you've come to offer your hand to my daughter?" He signed our volunteer applications and handed them back.

"Yes," said Teddy.

"We've come to offer your daughter a hand," I said. "To offer your hand means to get married," I explained to Teddy.

Teddy sat back a little. "I just want a place to practice the trumpet. The park is a very good place to do that."

Mayor Zimmerman laughed. "Well I'm glad you have your priorities in order."

"Does that mean that we can work at the park?" Teddy asked.

"Absolutely," said the mayor.

"Thanks," I said.

"No," said Mayor Zimmerman. "Thank you." He stood and glanced at his wristwatch. "I don't mean to be rude, but I have to run. I was just stopping in to grab some notes for my students."

"You're a teacher?" I asked.

"I teach business and finance at the community college. I've got a class in twenty minutes."

"Being mayor isn't your full-time job?"

"It's a full-time job all right."

"Do you get paid?" Teddy asked.

Mayor Zimmerman swept a handful of files and papers into a briefcase, then hurried us toward the door. "Ask Mrs. Robertson how much the mayor of Falls gets paid." We headed out of the mayor's office and back down the hall to the front counter. "Come back anytime, boys." He smiled at Teddy. "And let me know if you change your mind about marrying Pammy." With that, Mayor Z. left the building.

"Zero," Mrs. Robertson said once the city hall door swung shut.

"What?" I said.

"I listened to your conversation over the intercom," she told me. "Zero is how much the mayor gets paid."

"Zero's not a lot."

"It's even less than it used to be," said the Queen of Everything. While she spoke, Teddy and I unfolded our volunteer forms and filled in our names, addresses, and phone numbers. "Did the mayor sign your papers?"

"Yes, ma'am," said Teddy.

"You've got manners," Mrs. Robertson said to Teddy. "Your mother would be proud."

"Zachary has manners too," said Teddy.

"I'm sure his mother would also be proud."

Teddy turned to me. "Would she be proud, Zachary?"

I had no idea whether or not my mother would ever even learn about this good thing, and that made me suddenly very sad. But I knew that Teddy meant well so I forced a smile and nodded. "Sure."

"You know what?" Mrs. Robertson announced. "It doesn't really matter to me what either one of your mothers think. I'm the one that's lucky enough to be here with you right now."

"Thanks," I said.

"Thank you, both," she told us.

"You're welcome," said Teddy.

"Now," said Mrs. Robertson, "you can get out of my office."

Teddy and I must have both looked stunned, which made the Queen of Everything burst out laughing. "Are you going to stand around flirting with an old lady all day, or are you going to get yourselves to that park and help the mayor's daughter?"

Neither Teddy nor I responded.

"There's only one right answer!" She smiled. "Now get out of here!"

CHAPTER 11

Days went by, June turned into July, and Teddy and I found a sort of daily routine. I made sure to leave the kitchen door unlocked each night, and Teddy let himself in each morning. When I met him at the table, my hair sticking straight up and my eyes still half closed, he'd hop to his feet and shout, "Are you ready?"

On those mornings, that's when I really knew how far I'd traveled from our metal box trailer back in Colorado. Some days, I surprised myself by missing that place. I missed the simple kitchen and the straight-line highways and the sky interrupted by nothing but faraway mountains on the horizon. Falls was a more tangled-up kind of home. Everybody was connected. Everybody knew everyone. Family trees and street maps all looked like the chestnut and oak and maple branches that twisted around each other in the woods near Tilley's pond.

Occasionally, Dad found me and Teddy in the

kitchen during the mornings. We'd be eating breakfast or stealing a bread loaf to use later for the ducks
and to fish at the park. Dad always greeted Teddy
the same way. "Where y'at, Trumpet Boy?"

"Right here in your kitchen," Teddy replied.

"In New Orleans," Dad explained to Teddy,
"'Where y'at?' means 'How are you?'"

"Oh." Teddy was a little nervous around my
father, but I knew he liked it when Dad called him
Trumpet Boy.

"So, where y'at, Trumpet Boy?"

"Fine, thank you," said Teddy. "And you?"

"Let me see your horn," Dad said to Teddy one
morning.

Teddy pulled it out of his backpack and handed
it over. Dad examined the instrument carefully. "It's
a beauty."

"My father got it for me."

"You have a good dad."

"He should let me cook on the grill," said Teddy.
"He thinks I'm cooking-impaired."

My father struggled to keep a straight face. "Teddy,"
said Dad, "there are grills in the world that are not
located at the Falls Diner." He opened a cabinet above
our stove and reached up to a high shelf. He pulled a
trumpet mouthpiece down from the cabinet and
lifted Teddy's horn. "May I?"

Without waiting for a response, Dad removed

Teddy's mouthpiece from the trumpet and slipped his own into the brass tube. He licked his lips, then brought the instrument to his mouth. After a pause, Dad blew a long, clean note. Slowly, the sound grew and grew and grew. Suddenly, Dad turned the note into a big, wailing "Basin Street Blues."

"Wow!" said Teddy.

Dad lowered the horn and laughed. It was the first time I'd heard him really laugh in a long time.

"You're good," said Teddy.

"You're not so bad yourself."

Teddy grinned.

Dad turned to me. "How about you make supper for us tonight, Zachary?"

"Me?"

"Yes. And Trumpet Boy can help." He removed his mouthpiece and gave the horn back to Teddy. "I'll ask your father and sister to join us."

"Okay!" said Teddy, obviously excited. "But don't tell them I'm cooking."

"Why not?" I asked.

Teddy smiled. "I want to surprise them."

"I'll be home by six." Dad headed out of the house, leaving me alone in the kitchen with a very enthusiastic Trumpet Boy.

"What should we make for supper?" Teddy asked me.

"You want to talk about that now?"

"Now's good."

"Can we have breakfast first?"

Teddy headed toward the refrigerator and stopped in front of the door. He pointed to a small set of pictures that I'd stuck there the night before. "These are new."

"Not really." A couple magnets held a strip of photos that showed me, Mom, and Dad. We were sitting inside one of those old coin-op photo machines I remembered from a carnival somewhere. In the picture, I was five years old, my parents were happy, and that was a long, long time ago.

"Zachary," asked Teddy, "where is your mom?"

It was a simple question, but it took me by surprise. "I don't know."

"Is she dead like mine?"

"No."

Since the Panama Canal postcard, Dad and I had been receiving occasional short notes and pictures from various cruise ship destinations around the world. I knew they were from my mother, but it felt like we'd been selected to receive mail from a complete stranger. Dad always tossed the cards in the trash, but I rescued them and saved them in my room.

"Does she live in your old town?"

"I don't know where she lives, Teddy. My parents split up. My mom moved away."

"Why?"

I shrugged. "I don't know why."

"Did your parents love each other?"

I felt like somebody was hitting me in the head with a rolled-up towel. It didn't hurt, but I wasn't enjoying it. "What's with all the questions?"

"My dad still loves my mom," said Teddy, "even though she's gone."

I felt myself getting irritated. Was Teddy trying to compare my runaway mom with his dead mom? Dead moms would be simpler, wouldn't they? For example, Teddy didn't have to worry about his dead mom showing up out of the blue.

For a moment, I considered talking to Teddy about all the chaos going through my head, but honestly, this was not a conversation I really wanted to have with him. On the other hand, what did I want from Teddy? Did I want him to be like some kind of big dog who'd be devoted to me all the time just because that was his nature? Or did I want him to be a real person, somebody who asked hard questions that required answers I might not like.

"That's why he keeps her at the diner," Teddy said.

"What?"

"That's why my father keeps my mother at the diner. It's because he loves her so much."

"Like the Koza's with Coco the dog?"

Teddy looked surprised. "I never thought of it like that."

From the expression on his face, I saw that I had hurt his feelings. "I'm sorry," I said. "Your mother isn't like Coco the dog."

Teddy stood quietly examining the photos on the refrigerator. "Zachary," he said seriously, "my mother is dead, and she stays inside a store on Main Street. In some ways, she is like Coco the dog."

I tried to make him smile. "I bet she didn't have four legs and a furry face."

Teddy opened the refrigerator and took out a jar of peanut butter and a couple of apples. "I think about her a lot," he said, "but I don't remember as much as I used to. Sometimes I forget that Rachel never knew her." Teddy took a knife from the silverware drawer and a paper plate from a stack that Dad and I kept on the counter. He sliced the apples then smothered them with peanut butter. "It's like my sister and my mother are from two different families, and I'm supposed to be in both of them."

"You're the rope that holds them together," I suggested.

"If I'm the rope, then they're playing tug-of-war."

That made me laugh. "That's sort of how I feel about my mom and dad right now too."

"I don't like it."

I took a seat at the table. "I don't think there's any way to go back to the way it was before."

"Definitely not for me," said Teddy.

"Me neither."

Teddy went into a cabinet and found a box of Cheerios and a box of raisins. He poured cereal and raisins over the peanut butter apples then took a seat across from me and admired his special recipe.

"That looks disgusting," I said.

"But it tastes good."

I took a bite. "You're right," I admitted.

"Zachary," Teddy said seriously, "I think you have become much smarter since you came to Falls."

"Because I think you're right?"

Teddy nodded. "I think I am rubbing off on you."

I threw a Cheerio at him. "I am a better trumpet player than I used to be."

"That's because you practice."

"I guess you *are* rubbing off on me." I thought back to the evening in Copper Lake when my father played in the desert. It would be a long time before

I could make a trumpet sing like that. "You know," I said, "my dad makes up his own music."

Teddy took a handful of raisins. "I know it."

That surprised me. "Oh?"

"Sometimes I talk to him about the trumpet before you get out of bed in the mornings. He's working on a piece right now."

"He is?"

"I'm not supposed to talk about it," said Teddy.

"Why not?"

"It's a surprise."

"Does it have a name?" I asked.

Teddy looked worried. "I told your father that I am not good at keeping secrets."

"It's okay," I said. "You don't have to tell me."

"It's called *Zachary in B-flat*," Teddy burst out. "The name was my idea because he wants to make a song that's about you and that you are going to like and also because the trumpet is pitched in B-flat."

"Wow," I said.

"But I'm not going to tell you anything else, okay?"

"That's fine."

"You're sure?" Teddy asked.

"I'm positive."

"Good." We ate for a while without speaking until Teddy couldn't take it anymore.

"Zachary?"

"What?"

"Promise that you'll like it."

"I promise." Unlike the promise I'd made to Rachel, I had no doubt that this would be a pledge I could keep.

CHAPTER 12

WHEN HE GOT HOME THAT NIGHT, Dad found me and Teddy in the kitchen. "Have you boys been in here since breakfast?" he asked.

"I wish," I said.

"We had a very busy day," Teddy told my father. "We went to the park. We helped Pammy. We practiced the trumpet, then we got cookbooks at the library."

"I hear you visited Rachel in the kennel," said Dad.

Rachel was still volunteering with the police dogs even though she didn't have to anymore.

"We played fetch with Bert and Ernie," said Teddy. "Then we had lunch at the diner, and we had ice cream with Mr. Koza."

"Your day sounds busier than mine." Dad headed toward his bedroom to change his clothes.

"What did you do today?" Teddy called down the hallway.

"Bank robbers, gun fights, high speed chases, same old thing."

"He's kidding," I told Teddy. Then I shouted down the hall. "You're kidding, right?"

"Yes." Dad reappeared wearing a T-shirt and cut-off shorts. "What's for supper?"

"We went to the grocery store too," Teddy said.

Dad glanced at the pile of cookbooks still spread across the kitchen table. He looked impressed. "And?"

"And," I said, "Mrs. Koza sent us home with ice cream."

"We're not having ice cream for supper, are we?"

"Ice cream for dessert," said Teddy.

Dad lifted *The French Chef Cookbook* off the table and raised an eyebrow. "What did you make for supper?"

I grabbed a dish towel and started drying the pots and pans stacked in the sink. "I wanted to make something simple like hot dogs or chili."

"I like hot dogs and chili," Dad said.

"Teddy thought those were too easy."

"I wanted to make something good." Teddy broke open a new package of paper plates and started spreading them around the kitchen table.

Dad leaned against the counter and flipped through the French cookbook. "Easy is not the opposite of good."

I nodded toward Teddy. "I tried to tell him."

My father flipped through a few *French Chef Cookbook* pages. "Did you actually make one of these recipes?"

"We would have," I said, "if we knew what all the words meant."

"I found something good in one of the other books," said Teddy.

Dad raised an eyebrow. "*Qu'est-ce qui se?*"

I dropped my dish towel onto the counter, grabbed a book off the table and pointed to the picture on the cover. "Pistachio-crusted chicken with coconut chili ginger sauce."

"That's not simple."

"I like pistachios." Teddy put the extra plates on the counter and found a stack of napkins.

Dad sniffed the air. "But I don't smell pistachios or chicken or coconut or chili. I do smell—" He stopped suddenly and turned to me. "Zachary, was there a fire in here today?"

Just then, the doorbell rang. "Pizza's here!" said Teddy. "I'll get it!" He shoved the napkins into Dad's hands and ran out of the room.

"Pizza?" said Dad.

"It could have been worse," I told him.

Dad looked around. "At least you didn't burn down the kitchen."

"We tried. We couldn't even do that right."

"What happened?"

"I touched a dish towel on a hot burner," I confessed. "It was my fault. I dumped it in the sink right away. The fire only lasted a couple seconds."

Dad laughed. "It sounds like you two should have your own cooking show."

I grabbed the closest thing I could find—a clean dish towel—and threw it at my father. Dad caught it in midair. "Is this a pistachio-crusted dish towel?"

Before I could answer, Teddy came back into the kitchen carrying a pizza box. Rachel followed with another. Behind her, Mr. Spinelli carried one more.

"That's a lot of pizza," said Dad.

"We didn't know what you like," said Mr. Spinelli, "and leftover pizza never goes bad."

"You could have made pizza today," Dad whispered to Teddy when he put his box on the table.

Teddy shook his head. "Too easy."

Mr. Spinelli sniffed the air. "Was there a fire in here?"

"Let's eat!" Teddy nearly shouted at his father. "Officer Beatrice is hungry!"

"All right already," said his dad.

In a moment, the five of us were sharing paper plates and pizza. We didn't have enough chairs for everyone to fit around the table so I stood against the counter and took a random slice. It had pineapple on it, which I thought I'd hate but was actually pretty good.

"So how did you decide to move to Falls?" Mr. Spinelli asked my father.

"The job was here," Dad told him. "People seemed nice."

"And Zachary's mom wanted a change," Teddy offered through a mouthful of pizza. "But she didn't come here," he told his dad.

"Teddy," said Mr. Spinelli in a scolding voice, "that's none of our business."

Teddy looked hurt. "But that's what Zachary said."

"It's okay," said my father. "My ex-wife—" Dad glanced at me. "Zachary's mother—well, there's a lot of things she wanted to do, places she wanted to see. She didn't think she could have those things if she stayed married."

"Sorry to hear that," said Mr. Spinelli.

"Was she nice?" asked Teddy.

Dad's face grew tight. For just a moment, I thought he was going to tell the truth, that mom had been selfish and faithless and hurtful. Instead, he said, "Zachary's mom is funny and smart. She's the sort of person that other people want to be around. She's easy to like." I sighed and Dad shot me a look. "Those things are true," he said as if he could read my mind.

"She sounds a lot like Zachary," said Rachel.

That took me by surprise.

"Rachel's right," said Teddy, who must have noticed the look on my face.

"If Rachel likes you," Mr. Spinelli said to me, "then you must be easy to like."

"Who says I like him?" asked Rachel.

"Pammy says you like him," said Teddy.

I wasn't finished with the pizza on my plate, but I leaned over the table to take another piece and somehow whacked Teddy in the back of the head.

"Ouch!"

"What?" said Mr. Spinelli.

"Zachary bumped my head, and Rachel stepped on my foot."

"Sorry," I said.

"It was an accident," said Rachel.

"Zachary does take after his mother in some ways," Dad continued. "Except Zachary's mother likes to be the star of the show. She's always been the most important person in her life. Zachary is not like that."

"So your ex-wife is still back in Colorado?" Mr. Spinelli asked Dad.

"We don't really know, and we don't really care," I said. "She's the one who left us."

Dad held up a hand before I could say another

word. "We are not going to speak badly about your mother."

"Speaking badly about her would be a lot like telling the truth," I said.

"No," Dad said. "It wouldn't." He turned to Mr. Spinelli. "She drove away first, but I think she and I had already given up on each other in a lot of other ways."

"You would never just drive away," I said to Dad.

"That's true," he said. "I would have kept the three of us in that trailer long past the point of wanting to die." He reached across the table and took another piece of pizza. "I can't say that would be a better choice than the one your mother made."

"I'm glad you're here," said Teddy.

"So am I," said Dad.

"Do you think you'll ever see your mother again?" Rachel asked me.

I didn't respond. Dad cleared his throat. "Actually," he said, "she called a few days ago. She's planning to visit soon."

"What?" I turned so quickly that my pizza skidded off my plate and hit the floor with a *slap!*

"Zachary—" Dad said.

"When were you going to tell me?"

"I didn't have a chance when—"

"Are you excited?" Teddy said. "You must be really excited!"

"I'm—" I stopped. I didn't know how I felt. I had no idea what to expect or when it might happen. And I didn't have any idea what to say.

"Zachary," Dad said, "pick that pizza up off the floor."

I did as I'd been told, then I dumped the slice into the trash.

"Excuse me," I said after I wiped up the last of the tomato sauce. "I'm not hungry anymore."

With that, I left the room. For better or worse, nobody followed.

CHAPTER 13

FOR SEVERAL DAYS, I DID EVERYTHING I could to avoid my father. I stayed in bed till after he left for work. I spent as much time as possible helping out in the park, then coming home to eat supper in silence or, even better, alone. I spent most evenings reading horror novels in my bed, which inevitably led to nightmares involving zombies and vampires and poison ponds in the middle of some desert.

"Want to talk to me yet?" Dad asked late one night. He stood in my doorway, and I pretended that I'd fallen asleep with my face in a book.

"No," I muttered into my paperback.

"Your mother will be here soon."

"I don't care," I lied.

"Yes, you do."

"Why?" I said.

"Because she is your mother."

I lifted my head. "I mean, why is she coming?"

"Because," Dad said again, "she is your mother."

The next morning, I woke up to the sound of snoring from across the hall. It was still dark outside, but I decided to get dressed and out the door before Dad's alarm sounded. As quietly as possible, I tiptoed out of my room and into the kitchen. I grabbed a banana from the counter for breakfast, then reached for the back door. Just before I pulled it open, I heard, "Hey Zachary!"

I just about jumped out of my skin. Turning quickly, I saw Teddy sitting in the dark at the kitchen table. "What are you doing here?" I half whispered and half hollered at him. "You scared me!"

"Sorry," Teddy said.

The sun wasn't all the way up yet, but there was enough light to see that Teddy was as startled as me. "Are you always here this early?"

"Sometimes."

"But I won't be up for hours."

He shrugged. "I wait." Then he smiled. "But not today."

"Why not?"

"Because you're already awake, Zachary." Teddy nudged the backpack he'd placed on the floor. The bell of his trumpet stuck out the top. "We can get to the park early."

I shook my head. "Can we skip it today?"

Teddy looked confused. "Why?"

"I'm just not in the mood, okay?"

"When you don't want to practice, that's when you have to practice the most," said Teddy.

I tried and failed to keep the sarcasm out of my voice. "Thank you, Obi-Wan Trumpet Boy."

"You're welcome," said Teddy. "Are you ready to go?"

"No," I said sharply. "I don't want to."

"Rachel said you'd be upset."

"Did she?"

"Because your mom is coming," Teddy explained. "If I heard that my mother was coming, I'd be scared too, Zachary."

"That's because your mother is dead, Teddy. Everybody would be scared if they heard she was coming."

Teddy didn't respond at first. "That was mean," he finally said.

I took a deep breath. Then I turned to my friend. "You're right. I'm sorry."

"At least your mother can come and go."

"Sometimes I wish I could keep her stuck in a coffee can."

"It's a coffee pot," he said.

"What's the difference?"

"Your mother is not dead."

Teddy had a point. Even though I didn't want

to see my Mom, I didn't want her to be dead. But I also didn't want her to come to Falls. I didn't want her to sweep into this place that I'd started thinking of as my own town, my hometown, and ruin everything.

The door from outside swung open unexpectedly, and Rachel stepped into the kitchen. I glanced at the clock above the sink. It was past six, but not by much. "What are you doing here?"

"Good morning to you too," Rachel told me.

"Isn't this kind of early for you?"

"Just because I'm not here to greet you at every sunrise doesn't mean that I sleep till noon." Rachel was wearing the same basketball shorts and DOGZ ROOL T-shirt she had on when Teddy led us to the park for the first time at the beginning of summer.

"Are those your pajamas?" I asked.

"Yeah," said Rachel. "So?"

"She has Underdog, Clifford, and Charlie Dog pajamas too," said Teddy. "Rachel loves dogs," he added.

"Who's Charlie Dog?" I asked.

"You don't know Charlie Dog?" said Rachel.

I shook my head.

"He's in the Bugs Bunny cartoons sometimes. He's fifty percent collie, fifty percent Irish setter, fifty percent boxer, and fifty percent Doberman pinscher, but mostly, he's all Labrador retriever."

"He sounds like Skipper," I said.

106

Rachel crossed the kitchen and opened the refrigerator. "Do you have any orange juice?"

"We were just leaving," I told her.

"Now?" said Rachel. "Teddy told me that you always have breakfast before you go to the park. Did you already eat?"

"No," said Teddy. "Zachary and I had a fight."

Rachel closed the refrigerator door and gave me a sharp look. "Oh?"

"Zachary said our mother is dead."

Rachel looked confused. "Teddy, our mother is dead."

"And he said that she's in a coffee pot."

"Sorry to break it to you," Rachel told her brother, "but that's true too."

"He said it in a mean way," Teddy explained.

"I said I was sorry," I told him.

"He said he was sorry," Rachel repeated. "Can we get some breakfast now?"

Teddy considered me for a moment. "Okay," he finally said. "I forgive you."

"Excellent," said Rachel.

"Thanks," I said.

By then, the sun was brighter in the sky. Light flowed into the kitchen, and I could hear Dad starting to move around at the end of the hall. I still didn't want to talk to him yet. "Can we eat at the diner?" I asked.

"Will you bring your trumpet?" Teddy asked me.

"Fine," I said. "I'll bring it."

Teddy stood. "Then let's go to the diner."

A few minutes later, the three of us were seated around a corner table beneath a bright circus poster at the Falls Diner. "Look who's here," Mr. Spinelli said when we came into the restaurant. "It's the breakfast club."

"No," Teddy told his father. "It's the trumpet club."

"Even better." Mr. Spinelli ducked into the kitchen. He returned a little while later with huge stacks of pancakes, maple syrup, and a pitcher of orange juice. "Dig in."

"Thanks," we said.

Rachel attacked her breakfast as if she hadn't eaten for days. I did my best, but I ended up sliding a couple untouched pancakes from my plate onto Teddy's. He finished them off quickly. Rachel pointed a fork at her brother. "I don't know where he puts it."

I gestured at her empty plate. "You should talk."

She gave me a big grin, stuck a finger into the puddle of syrup still on my plate, and licked it off.

I leaned back and stared at the green and white carousel horse suspended above us. The animal's expression was fierce and wild. Emerald- and ruby-colored stones studded a gold saddle on its back, and a real leather halter led to a metal bit stuck between its teeth. "Is that real?" I asked.

Teddy glanced up. "It's wood," he said matter-of-factly.

Rachel must have noticed the confused look on my face. "It's a wooden horse. Not a real horse that's stuffed. But that's not what you're asking, is it?"

I shook my head. "Is it a real carousel horse? Was it ever part of a real merry-go-round?"

Rachel nodded. "It came from the merry-go-round at Tilley's Park."

"There's a merry-go-round at the park?"

"There used to be," said Teddy.

"What happened to it?" I asked.

Rachel poured herself a glass of juice. "Dad says there used to be a bunch of carnival rides at the park. They were all gone before we were born." She pointed at the carved horse above us. "Dad found this one in an antique shop. He swears that he remembers our mom riding it when she was a little girl."

"Our mom loved the rides," said Teddy. "And she loved the park."

"Your mom sounds like she was nice," I said.

Rachel shrugged. "I guess."

"She was," said Teddy, whose attention wandered

to the silver coffee pot above the cash register. "I hope she's comfortable in there."

Rachel and I turned toward the coffee pot. "Are you ever going to let her out?" I asked after a moment.

"What do you mean?" said Teddy.

"I don't know. I never realized you could keep somebody's ashes—"

"In a coffee pot?" said Rachel.

"I never realized you could keep them at all. I thought you just kept ashes in containers until you decided upon a final resting place."

"You don't think downtown Falls is a good final resting place?" asked Rachel.

"I'm sure there are worse places," I said.

"Our mother is not really inside the coffee pot," said Rachel.

Teddy turned toward his sister. He looked a little alarmed. "Then who's in there?"

"Nobody is in there," said Rachel. "It's just ashes."

"What exactly are ashes?" Teddy asked.

Rachel gave her brother a cautious look. "Didn't Dad ever talk to you about this?"

Teddy looked at her blankly.

"We've been looking at the coffee pot for our whole lives," Rachel told her brother. "Haven't you ever thought about what's really in there?"

He shrugged. "No."

"Teddy," I said, "when people die . . . well, they're not alive anymore."

He gave me an annoyed look. "I know that, Zachary."

"I mean that their bodies are still here, but they're not—"

"They're not alive," said Teddy. "I get it."

"You can't keep a dead body lying around." Rachel glanced around the room. "Not in a restaurant anyway."

"Sometimes we bury them," I explained.

"At cemeteries," said Teddy.

I nodded. "Sometimes we burn them."

Teddy looked confused. "Like in a fireplace?"

I thought about it. "I don't actually know where they burn them." I glanced at Rachel. "Do you?"

She shrugged. "A body burning place? Tanning salons? I don't know."

I turned back to Teddy. "You know how there's ashes in a fireplace after you burn logs in the fire?"

"Yeah."

"Well," I said, "there's ashes left over when you're done burning a body."

"But that's like dirt," said Teddy.

"I guess," I said.

"Why are we keeping dirt?" Teddy said to his sister.

Rachel didn't answer.

Teddy stood. He glanced quickly around the diner. A few of the tables and booths held people from around town. Mr. Spinelli was back in the kitchen so he didn't see what happened next. Teddy crossed the room, took the coffeepot down from the shelf, then returned to his seat at our table.

"What are you doing?" Rachel said in a shocked whisper.

Teddy shook the percolator. Something that sounded like sand bounced around inside. "Is this dirt or is this Mom?" he asked his sister.

"I don't know," Rachel replied sharply. "Neither. Both. What does it matter?"

"It matters!" Teddy stood again. "If it's just dirt"—he lowered his voice—"then we're like crazy people. If it's Mom—" He took a breath. "I want to let her out!"

Before Rachel or I could react, Teddy grabbed his backpack, stuffed the coffeepot inside of it alongside his trumpet, and then he sprinted out the door. Through the restaurant's front windows, we saw him hop onto his bicycle and pedal away.

"Don't just sit there!" Rachel yelled at me. Her cheeks were flush with anger.

"What do you want me to do?"

People inside the restaurant turned toward us.

"I don't know! This is your fault. Go after him!"

"My fault?"

"You told him to let her out."

"I did not!"

"Just go!" Rachel shouted.

"What's going on out there?" called Mr. Spinelli from the kitchen.

Rachel and I exchanged terrified looks. "NOTHING!" we shouted back.

"Listen," Rachel lowered her voice. "I'll give my father some story about the coffeepot, then I'll catch up with you. Now go."

"Where am I going?" I said.

"To the park!" She nearly spat in my face. "Didn't you hear what Teddy said? My mother loved the park. She rode the stupid merry-go-round. She used to bring Teddy there when he was a toddler."

"What about you?"

"She was already dead when I was a toddler."

"I mean how are you going to get to the park?

"I'll figure something out. Just go!"

I retrieved my bicycle from the front of the diner and pedaled as if I were being chased by a pack of characters from the horror novels stacked around my bed. I got to the park in no time and dropped my bike at the edge of the pond.

The water was smooth as polished steel until a fish jumped and broke the surface. I wondered where the fish came from since this had been nothing more than a mud pit a few months earlier. Now it was bursting with life.

"Helloooooo!" I hollered. My voice carried across the pond's surface, then echoed off the hill above the opposite shore. Otherwise, there was no answer. I shouted again. "Helloooooo!"

This time, my call was answered with a splash that sounded much louder than seemed possible for a fish or frog to make. A circle of waves spreading across the pond showed me the spot on the water where the noise must have come from. At the center of that circle, a shiny metal coffee pot bobbed up and down. Teddy stood at the shore not too far away. I left my bike behind and jogged to his side.

"What are you doing?" I asked.

He pointed to the coffee pot. "It floats."

"Probably not for long," I told him.

"You said she needed a final resting place."

"I didn't mean today."

Teddy didn't reply.

"If you're going to put your mother in her final resting place, don't you think your father and sister would want to help?"

"They could have done it a long time ago." His voice echoed angrily across the water.

The two of us stared at the little pot still bouncing along on the ripples.

"She's been at the diner for a long time," I said.

Teddy did not turn away from the water. "But she's been gone for a long time too."

"It's hard to say goodbye," I said.

"I didn't want her to leave," Teddy told me.

I closed my eyes. "I know."

Teddy pointed at the coffee pot bobbing along. It had drifted twenty or thirty feet away from the shore. "But it doesn't make any sense, Zachary. It's just silly. Why would you put a person in a coffee pot?"

I shook my head. "I honestly don't know."

Teddy sighed. He sat in the grass and started to untie his shoes.

"What are you doing?" I asked.

"You're right," he said. "I shouldn't do this without my dad and my sister. I better get Mom out of the pond."

"Wait," I told him. "You're going to be in enough trouble without coming home all covered in mud. Let me."

Teddy hesitated.

"Please," I told him. "It will just take a second." Before he could answer, I kicked my own shoes off and stepped into the pond. My toes sunk into mud that was soft and cool. "Just stay there," I told Teddy. "I'll be right back." I waded forward. The water rose past my knees and then up to my waist. The cold made me gasp a little.

"Are you okay?" Teddy called from the shore.

"I'm fine." I glanced ahead and saw that the coffee pot had floated even farther away. The stream that trickled in from the hill must have created a small, steady current that was pushing it toward the opposite shore. I realized that we could have just walked around to the other side and waited for the current to push the pot to the water's edge, but I was in too deep to go back now.

I took another step forward and hit an unexpected drop. I shot down quickly and water went over my head. It was a surprise, but I wasn't worried until suddenly, a huge blast of water and bubbles exploded around me. Then two strong hands grabbed my hair and ears. They yanked me back to the surface, and dragged me toward the shore. "What the—"

"Are you all right?" Teddy shouted in my face.

"Put me down!" I yelled.

He released me so that I was standing in waist deep water again. "What happened?" Teddy asked in a panicked voice.

"Nothing," I said. "The water just got deeper. I slipped."

"It looked like something pulled you under," he said breathlessly. "I saved you!"

I wanted to laugh, but it was clear that Teddy was really scared. "I'm okay," I told him.

"You have to be careful near water!"

"I know," I said.

"I saved you," he said again.

"Okay," I said. "You saved me."

Just then, we heard Rachel's voice. "What do you think you're doing?"

We hadn't even noticed her arrive. Now she stood on the shore yelling at Teddy and me.

"How did you get here?" I called.

She bent over and put her hands on her knees. "I ran."

"After all those pancakes?" I said.

She raised her head and gave me a dirty look.

"It's okay," I told her. "Teddy just saved me."

"Teddy," said Rachel breathlessly, "doesn't know how to swim."

I turned to Teddy. "You don't?"

Teddy shook his head. "No."

"And you jumped in after me?"

"You needed me," Teddy said simply.

"You are my hero," I said, "but don't do that again, okay?"

Teddy grinned from ear to ear. Strands of pond scum and weeds hung from his shoulders, and his face and hair were dappled with mud.

"Get out of the water," Rachel yelled at him.

"You get out." Being a hero had Teddy feeling pretty full of himself.

Rachel stood up straight. "I'm not in the water. And look at you. You're filthy."

"Hey," I said to Rachel. "He just saved my life. Give him some credit."

"Yeah," said Teddy. "Give me some credit. I'm not retarded."

Rachel's head shot up. "I did not say that."

"You act like it," Teddy said.

Rachel's face turned scarlet. "I do not."

"Sometimes you do," Teddy yelled at his sister.

I put my hand out to Teddy. "Easy does it there, hero."

"Take that back!" Rachel shouted at him.

"No," said Teddy.

Rachel looked around like she was trying to find something to throw. She picked up a good size rock. "Take it back!"

"No!" Teddy said again.

Rachel totally lost it. She wound up and threw the stone at her brother as hard as she could. Without thinking, I dragged Teddy back into the water. He splashed into the pond and the stone skipped harmlessly away.

"What are you doing?" I yelled at Rachel.

She let out a sound that was half growl and half lion's roar. Before she got to full carnivorous rage, however, she stopped. A panicked look crossed her face. "Teddy!" she screamed.

I looked around. Teddy had not resurfaced.

Rachel charged into the pond. I dove into the spot where I saw Teddy last. I left my eyes wide open beneath the water, but we'd stirred up too much mud. I couldn't see a thing. I thrashed my arms and legs around until I felt flesh. I grabbed what I hoped was Teddy's arm and pushed up with all my might. I burst out of the water, and by the time I gulped down a mouthful of air, Teddy was standing beside me.

"What happened?" I gasped.

"Rachel threw a rock at me."

"I know that. What happened to you?"

"I sat down under the water. I held my breath."

"You what?" I said.

"I sat in the mud. It felt good."

"I thought—" I glanced at Rachel who stood in ankle deep water with a stunned look on her face. "We thought—"

Teddy pointed at his sister. "She thinks I'm retarded."

"She does not," I said.

"She does too." Teddy raised a fist. It was filled with a handful of mud and muck scooped from the bottom of the pond. "You do too!" he hollered at his sister. Then he flung the smelly mess at Rachel. It splattered across her face and clothes.

"Stop it!" I yelled.

But nothing I shouted was going to stop him. Teddy raised his other hand. This one had even more mud than the first.

"Run!" I yelled at Rachel.

She backed away from the edge of the water and headed toward the trees. Teddy leaned back and chucked the dripping dirt with all his might. His throw went high, and it sailed into the branches above Rachel's head. Somehow, the whole gloppy mess stuck together and smacked into a spindly set of twigs and leaves, an old squirrel's nest, that tipped, swayed, and finally dropped on Rachel's head.

"Rachel!" I yelled.

"Teddy!" Rachel roared.

"Squirrel!" Teddy hollered back.

"What?" I said.

Teddy pointed. Apparently, the squirrel nest wasn't as old as it looked. It contained a real live squirrel. The bushy-tailed rodent sat up on Rachel's head and looked around in a panic. "Squirrel!" Teddy said again. "A big one!"

"GET IT OFF!" Rachel screamed.

Teddy and I sprung toward Rachel. We tried to sprint, but water is heavy, and we were standing in it up to our necks. Fortunately, the splashing and screaming and commotion were enough to convince the wild beast on Rachel's head to leap away. It scrambled deep into the woods before Teddy and I even reached the shore.

"We saved you!" Teddy hollered when we finally got to Rachel.

I started to laugh. "We saved you from a squirrel!"

The next thing I knew, I was lying on my back. There was a ringing in my ears, and my right eye was swelling shut.

"She punched you," Teddy said from somewhere above.

I sat up. "I noticed." I looked around. "Where did she go?"

Teddy pointed at the woods. Rachel was stomping away through the trees and out of sight.

I struggled to my feet. "What just happened?" I asked Teddy.

"I told you, Zachary. She punched you."

"I know that part," I said. "But why?"

Teddy shrugged. "Sometimes she just goes crazy."

I touched my cheek lightly. "It must run in the family."

Teddy looked embarrassed.

"You and your sister are not so different."

"You're going to have a black eye," he told me.

I touched my face again. The throbbing spread across my forehead and down my cheek.

"You should put a bag of frozen peas on your face when you get home," Teddy told me.

"It might be too late for that."

"It won't hurt to try."

"Teddy," I said. "I think it's going to hurt no matter what I do."

CHAPTER 14

TEDDY LIFTED HIS BIKE OFF THE GRASS. The two of us walked around the edge of the pond until we found the coffee pot bobbing in a knee-deep pool near the water's edge. A couple small perch swam up from their round, gravelly nest to poke and prod at the shiny thing. Teddy found an old branch long enough to stick through the coffee pot's handle and lift it out of the water. He shook it, and the insides still sounded sandy and dry.

"How about we bring your mom back to the diner," I suggested.

Teddy sighed. "My father's going to be mad."

I couldn't lie. "Probably."

"I was just trying to do the right thing."

"What do you mean?" I asked.

"I think it's time to put my mom in a better place."

I put a hand on Teddy's shoulder. "I don't think you can do that by yourself."

"No."

Teddy and I pedaled back to the diner where we found Mr. Spinelli waiting for us on the sidewalk. "Thank you for bringing Teddy back," he said to me.

"I didn't bring him back. We came back together." I turned to my muddy friend. "I'm going home to wash up. I'll see you later."

He glanced at his father and then to me. "I hope so."

Mr. Spinelli nodded toward my face. "How did you get the black eye?"

Neither Teddy nor I spoke.

"Did you two get into a fight?"

"No," said Teddy.

"I got into a fight with a squirrel," I said.

Mr. Spinelli raised an eyebrow. "It looks like the squirrel won."

I nodded. "We didn't have squirrels like yours back in Colorado. I'll be ready next time."

Mr. Spinelli gave me a careful look. "Do you want to tell me what really happened?"

"Teddy will tell you," I said.

"Will he?" said Mr. Spinelli.

"Just the parts that matter," I said.

Mr. Spinelli turned to his son. "Should we go inside?"

Teddy dropped his backpack off his shoulder and held it close against his stomach. "Okay."

From there, I headed away from Main Street and pedaled back toward home. I found Rachel sitting on the curb near the end of my driveway.

"I'm sorry," Rachel said before I was even off my bike.

I put the bike in the grass and sat down beside her.

"How's your eye?" she asked.

"It hurts," I admitted, "but I'm not blind."

"You must be. If you could see, you would have noticed me and then kept going."

I lay back and stared at the fat clouds scudding across the sky. "I saw you."

"Then why'd you stop?"

"We're friends," I said. "Plus, you're sitting in front of my house."

She pulled her knees up to her chest, wrapping her arms around her legs. "Friends don't punch friends in the face."

I sat up. "Sure they do."

"Really?"

"Only the very best friends."

"Are we best friends?" Rachel asked.

I didn't answer.

"Teddy says that he's your best friend."

"You can have more than one best friend," I told her.

"How's that?"

"You can have a best boy friend, a best girl friend—"

"Am I your girlfriend?"

I shifted in the grass. "That's not what we were talking about."

"My brother collects best friends like some people collect wishbones."

"Wishbones?" I said. "Like the ones you find inside chickens?"

"They're inside turkeys too."

"People collect those?"

"Some people do."

"I'd rather collect friends," I told her.

"Wishbones are easier." Heat from the day rose up from the black tar at our feet. "Can I ask you something, Zachary?"

I picked up a pebble and tossed it into the road. "Ask away."

"I know you like me."

"That's not a question," I pointed out.

"Some boys think I'm pretty," she continued.

I found another pebble. "You *are* pretty."

"I don't care about that."

I stared up at a cloud that looked like a unicorn playing a saxophone. "Okay," I said.

"Sometimes boys think I'll like them if they're nice to Teddy," Rachel went on.

The summer sun felt like it was pressing hard

against the top of my head, and a bad feeling started to work its way up through my feet like the temperature from the blacktop. "Are you asking me if I'm friends with Teddy just so I can hang out with you?"

"I'm saying that it's happened before."

"It's not happening now."

"Okay," Rachel nodded. "I'm glad."

I suppose that should have made me feel better, but it didn't. I was hot, the pain in my eye had spread across the whole right side of my face, and I smelled like pond scum. "Well hurray for you."

Rachel shoved me hard in the shoulder. "I mean it."

"Listen," I told her. "Teddy is my friend. And guess what else?"

"What?" she asked.

My voice was getting louder, and I couldn't help it. In fact, I didn't want to help it. "I look out for my friends," I said. "And you could have a face like a scab or you could be Miss America, and I'd still think you're pretty, okay?"

"Okay."

"So get over yourself, because believe it or not, not everything is about you."

Rachel leaned away from me. "I do not think that everything is about me."

"Yes, you do. And if you don't like what somebody is saying, then you punch them in the face."

Rachel's expression turned stony. "I punched you in the face because you were making fun of me."

"Look what you did at the pond just now." I should have stopped but I couldn't. "Teddy and I pulled your mom's ashes out of the water. Your brother thought he saved me from drowning. You came along and yelled at him for getting wet."

"I yelled at him because he can't swim!"

"You yelled because you wanted everybody to know that you're the boss. Teddy does not need you to be the boss. And by the way, I was not making fun of you. I was laughing at you."

"Big difference," said Rachel.

"You had a squirrel on your head!" I shouted. "That's funny!"

"It wasn't funny to me!"

"Then you should lighten up. And by the way, I don't think you meant to hit me in the first place."

"I meant to hit you," said Rachel. "Right now, I wouldn't mind hitting you again."

"You punched me because you were mad at your brother. You wanted to hit Teddy, but you would never do that. Your brother is the size of a buffalo, but sometimes you treat him like some kind of sickly ballerina."

"First of all," Rachel said through gritted teeth, "ballerinas are tough. Second of all, I threw a rock at my brother. That wasn't enough for you?"

"I mean no disrespect to ballerinas," I said. "And you missed Teddy on purpose."

"I did not."

"Yes you did. You act like he's . . ."

Rachel's glare stopped me mid-sentence.

"You treat him like he's a little kid."

Rachel didn't answer.

"He's not a toddler," I said.

Rachel turned to face me. She took a big breath before she spoke. "You say everything is about me. It's not. Everything is about Teddy. Every day is looking out for Teddy. You know, there have been days this summer when I would have liked to hang out with you, Zachary. But that's not possible. Teddy is always there."

"You could come with us," I said.

"Oh my God!" she yelled. "Listen to me. I would like to spend time with you, Zachary. Just you and just me. Alone. Together. Get it?"

"Oh," I said.

"But that's not going to happen because between the two of us, we are with Teddy all the time. Even when he's not around, I have to think of Teddy every second of every day."

"No you don't," I told her.

"Who else is going to do it? Who else is going to look out for him?" Rachel shouted at me.

"Teddy can look out for himself sometimes," I

said. "And what about asking for help? What about your father?"

Rachel stood. "My father? My father works all the time. He lives at the diner! He says he does it so that we'll have money for me to go to college, but sometimes it just feels like he doesn't want to be around. And how am I supposed to go to college anyway? I don't even know if I want to go to college. And if I go, what then? What will happen to Teddy when I leave? Who will take care of him?" She sat down hard back onto the grass.

"That's a lot of questions," I said after a little time had passed.

"I could use some answers," said Rachel.

"Is that why you get so mad?" I asked.

"Do you mean now or all the time?"

I shrugged. "Both."

"I love my brother, Zachary. I really do. But I don't want to be his babysitter for the rest of my life."

"Your brother is not stupid, Rachel."

"I know that."

"My father says he's brilliant," I added. "But he is different from other people. He's special. In a good way."

Rachel sighed.

"He'll always need you, but—"

"But what?" It sounded almost like Rachel might cry.

"I don't think he needs you to be his babysitter for the rest of his life."

Rachel slid over so that she was sitting right beside me. We both stared across the street at her house. "Then what will I be?" she asked.

"You will be his sister," I said.

Rachel leaned her head against my shoulder. I tried to think what I would want me to do if I was her right now. In movies, this would be the part where the boy kissed the girl, but I'd already been thumped in the face once today. I did not want to risk another black eye. Also, the smell of fish and frogs hung in the air between us. It just did not seem like a kiss-the-girl kind of moment. Instead, I put my arm around Rachel and bit my tongue so I would not say anything stupid. Then we sat that way for a long, long time.

CHAPTER 15

Dad FOUND ME AT THE KITCHEN TABLE when he got up the next morning. "Where's Trumpet Boy?" he asked.

I kept my face low and close to my cereal bowl in the hope that Dad wouldn't see my black eye. "He got in trouble yesterday."

"What happened?"

I took a breath. "Teddy stole the coffee pot that's filled with his dead mother's ashes and threw it into the pond at Tilley's park."

Dad pulled a loaf of bread from the refrigerator and plugged in the toaster. "So it was another busy day for you two."

"You could say that."

"Is that how you got that shiner?"

I lifted my head. "It had something to do with it," I admitted.

"I see," said Dad.

"You do?" I asked.

"Not really." He shoved a couple slices into the toaster and went back to the refrigerator for butter and jelly.

"We pulled the coffee pot out of the pond," I told him. "Teddy's mom is back at the diner."

"Safe and sound?" asked Dad.

"Dry as a bone."

Dad opened his mouth to respond, but the toaster popped before he could speak. I took the opportunity to keep on talking.

"I think Teddy might be grounded for a couple days."

Dad grabbed the hot toast and flung it onto a napkin. "That's understandable." He carried his breakfast to the table and sat down across from me. "So?"

"So what?" I asked.

Dad spread butter and jelly onto the bread. "So," he said, "what are we going to do about your mother?"

I didn't answer.

"We can't stuff her in a coffee pot and throw her in a pond." Dad took a bite of toast and chewed slowly.

"We could try," I muttered.

"It didn't work for Teddy and Rachel."

"It's a very different situation," I said.

"True," said Dad.

"Does she have to come here?" I asked.

"She's coming," he told me.

I stood and carried my cereal bowl toward the kitchen sink. "Why?" I asked. "Why now? We didn't invite her."

"Actually . . ." said Dad.

"What?"

Dad didn't speak for a moment.

"Did you tell her to come?"

He sighed. "I suggested it."

I stopped so quickly that the bowl slipped out of my hand. I went to grab for it, but instead, I knocked the thing into the edge of the counter. It flipped over, then sailed toward the center of the kitchen. For one long, slow-motion moment, I recalled the nursery rhyme about the dish running away with the spoon. I wondered if my bowl was trying to fly away. If so, it didn't get far. Instead, it smashed into the floor and shattered into a billion pieces.

"Don't move," Dad told me.

"I'm fine," I said.

"You have bare feet."

"Why did you tell her to come here?"

Dad stood trapped between my question and the broom closet. "Wait," he said. "I can only deal with one crisis at a time." He opened the closet and retrieved a broom and dustpan.

"The dish comes first?" I asked.

Dad ignored me and knelt to sweep up the shards.

134

He concentrated on the broken pieces as if each one was a small land mine.

"Why didn't you tell me?" I said.

He stood and carried the dustpan toward the garbage. "You've been avoiding me for days, Zachary. When was I going to tell you?"

"How about before you asked her to come?"

Dad dumped the broken bowl into the trash then turned to face me. "First of all," he said, "I don't need to check in with you about my contact with your mother. Second of all, I'm not the one who wants to see her."

"What are you talking about?"

"I saw the postcards you shoved in the bottom of your sock drawer."

"What are you doing in my sock drawer?" I yelled.

"I do the laundry, Zachary. I put your socks away."

That deflated me a little. "Oh."

Dad went over the floor one more time with the broom while I stayed in my spot by the sink. "It's okay if you want to see her," he finally said.

"I don't want to see her."

"You don't know what you want."

I wanted to disagree. But I couldn't.

"Your mother and I said our good-byes," Dad told me. "It wasn't pretty, and it dragged on way too long. I understand why she snuck out the way she did, but that wasn't fair to you." He tucked the broom back where it belonged. "It wasn't fair to anybody."

"She shouldn't have run away."

"She was just worn out."

"Why?"

Dad took a seat back at the table. "She had such big plans," he said. "She was going to inherit a thousand acres then sell it to get rich. She meant to marry a big time musician then travel around the world mixing and mingling with artists and superstars. It never quite worked out the way she wanted."

"Wasn't there anything you could do?"

Dad hesitated. "If you're asking me if your mother is the only one to blame for what happened, Zachary, then the answer is no. She and I hurt each other, and we hurt you too. That's both our faults, and I'm sorry. If you're asking me if I could have done something to make her happy, I honestly have no idea."

"Oh."

"She was going crazy, and she was dragging us there too. It had to end. I give her a lot of credit for making it stop."

"But if she stayed, maybe things would have gotten better."

"No, Zachary."

"You don't know that."

"Seeing the future is one of my superpowers," Dad said. "Remember?"

"When am I going to get some of these superpowers you're always talking about?

"Zachary," Dad said, "you've got more than you know."

"Predict our future now," I told him.

Dad sighed. "Things are a little cloudy at the moment."

"You can do better than that."

He gave me a tired look. "Okay." My father closed his eyes and bowed his head almost as if he were about to say a prayer. "In the future," he said, "I smell good food. I hear great music. I feel joy and chaos in equal measure." He opened his eyes. "How's that?"

"It's weak."

Dad shut his eyes again. "I also can see you very clearly, Zachary. I see that no matter what happens, no matter what you do, no matter where you go . . . I will always be here for you."

Before he could open his eyes, I took two giant steps to cross the kitchen. My father must have heard me coming because he opened his arms wide, and I let him wrap me into a giant hug. I know that I was much too old for that sort of thing, but in the face of Dad's superpowers, I could not resist. And I did not want to.

CHAPTER 16

The following afternoon, I pedaled downtown with my trumpet stuffed into the backpack slung over my shoulder. I hadn't seen Teddy or Rachel at home, so I hoped I'd find them at the diner. Rolling down Main Street, I glanced into Coco's Cones and saw Mrs. Yee, even more pregnant than when we'd seen her on the last day of school. She waved me inside so I parked my bike, gave Coco a pat on the head, and entered the shop.

"Zachary!" Mrs. Yee shouted. "*Dzien dobry!*"

"I didn't know you were Polish," I said.

"Everybody is Polish when you're in Coco's Cones," she told me.

"Then *dzien dobry* to you too."

She pointed at my face. "What happened to your eye?"

It was too hard to explain so I pointed at her tummy. "You're really big."

Mr. Koza, who was sitting at his table and reading

the newspaper, laughed out loud. Mrs. Yee turned to face him. "What's so funny, Ice Cream Man?"

Mr. Koza chuckled. "Was I ever so young and dumb?"

"Yes!" Mrs. Koza called from behind the counter.

"Zachary," Mrs. Yee said with a forced grin. "A pregnant woman who is three weeks past her due date does not need to hear, 'You are really big.'"

"You were supposed to have the baby three weeks ago?"

"I'm a medical miracle."

"I just meant that you are usually a very small person, and you're still pretty even when you're not. I mean not small."

Mrs. Koza came out from behind the counter. She shoved a bowl of ice cream into my hand and stuck a cookie in my face. "Put the cookie into your mouth, Zachary. Maybe it will stop the flow of words before it is too late."

"But—"

Mrs. Yee laughed. "I accept your compliment, Zachary. Now take Mrs. Koza's advice before I make your other eye black."

I bit the cookie. It was good.

"And the ice cream," Mrs. Koza told me.

"Okay." I scooped ice cream into my mouth. The taste wasn't at all what I expected. The surprise must have shown on my face.

"It is *krem z herbaty*," said Mrs. Koza.

"Krem what?" I said.

"*Krem* like cream. *Herbaty* is herbal tea."

"Herbal tea ice cream?"

"Exactly," said Mrs. Koza.

"It was my favorite when I was a boy," said Mr. Koza. "It is very popular in Poland."

"He has been bothering me about it for years, but I could never get the recipe just right," Mrs. Koza explained. "Until today. You are first person to try it, Zachary. Do you like?"

"I do."

Mrs. Koza beamed. "Good."

"What did I tell you?" Mr. Koza told his wife. "It will be very popular."

"You tell me so many things," said Mrs. Koza. "Something will turn out to be right eventually."

I studied the couple. To me, they looked like the little old man and the little old woman from an old picture book called *Millions of Cats*. Dad used to read it out loud to me when I was small. My favorite part was a set of repeating lines, like a refrain, that we would recite together at the top of our lungs. *Hundreds of cats, thousands of cats, millions and billions and trillions of cats!* "Shut up about the cats!" Mom would scream at us.

"Zachary," Mrs. Yee called. She had a big ice cream cone, and she'd lowered herself into a chair near the wall. "Come join me."

140

I backed away from the old couple and pulled up a seat with my teacher. She nodded toward Mr. and Mrs. Koza. "I hope my husband and I will be just like them one day."

"They're a little crazy," I whispered.

"We are all a little crazy." Mrs. Yee pointed at my eye again. "Are you going to tell me what happened?"

"I'd rather not."

"Tell me anyway."

I sighed. "Rachel Spinelli punched me in the face."

Mrs. Yee raised an eyebrow. "Did you deserve it?"

"I laughed when a squirrel fell on her head."

"Well, there's something you don't see every day."

A picture appeared in my head of the bushy-tailed rodent landing in Rachel's hair. I bit back a smile. "No."

Mrs. Yee reached out and touched my face. "She must have been pretty upset to give you that black eye."

"She was."

"A squirrel really fell on her head?"

I nodded. "He looked like a circus animal standing on a ball."

Mrs. Yee's mouth turned into a smile. "What else could you do besides laugh?"

"I guess I could have ducked."

"At least you know what to do the next time it happens." She pointed at the trumpet sticking out of the backpack I'd placed on the floor. "Have you been practicing?"

"Lots," I told her, happy to change the subject. "Teddy's been helping me."

"That's good."

Mrs. Yee took a bite from her cone. I glanced down at her stomach. "May I put my hand on your tummy?"

"Sure," she said. "You can tell people you know what it's like to touch the moon." She reached over, took my wrist, and stretched my arm across the table. Then she placed my hand across the front of her shirt. At first, there was nothing. Then out of nowhere, I felt the baby give a huge kick beneath my hand.

"Ooof!" Mrs. Yee sat up quickly in her chair.

"Wow!" I said.

"Uh-oh." Mrs. Yee suddenly looked a little dazed.

Mrs. Koza must have noticed something change because she rushed over to our table. "What is it?" she asked.

"The baby kicked," I said.

Mrs. Yee took a breath. "I think it's time."

"Time for what?" I asked.

Mrs. Yee laughed out loud. "The baby is coming!"

"No way," I said.

"Way," said Mrs. Yee. She pushed herself into a standing position. "Mr. Koza, could you drive me to the—" She stopped mid-sentence and closed her eyes tight. After a moment passed, she said, "—hospital?"

Mr. Koza hopped up a lot more quickly than I would have guessed possible. "Yes! Yes, of course!" He didn't move away from the table.

"Now?" asked Mrs. Yee.

"I can do that!" said Mr. Koza.

Mrs. Koza turned and shouted at her husband. "Then you will need to get the car!"

"I will get the car!" Mr. Koza announced as if the idea had just occurred to him. He rushed out the door.

Mrs. Yee shoved what was left of her ice cream cone into my hands then dug a cell phone out of her purse. "I'm going to call my husband. I'll tell him to meet us at the—" Again she paused and closed her eyes for a moment. A look of pain crossed her face, and then she finished the sentence. "—hospital."

"Please don't say hospital again!" I blurted out.

Mrs. Yee laughed so hard that tears started to run down her cheeks. "It has nothing to do with the word—" She stopped then clutched my arm so tightly I thought my knees would buckle. "—hos—"

"Don't say it!" I shouted.

She released my arm. "I was just kidding that time."

A moment later, a big, orange station wagon

roared to a stop in front of the ice cream shop. Mr. Koza hopped out and opened the back door. Mrs. Koza and I guided Mrs. Yee to the car while she spoke to her husband on the cell phone. "Meet me as soon as you can! I'm going straight to the"—she looked at me then broke into a fit of giggles—"the baby delivery place." She snapped the phone shut, then leaned forward and kissed me on the cheek. "Thank you, Zachary."

"For what?" I said, surprised at her kiss.

"For being here. For making me laugh." She backed into the station wagon, pulled the car door shut, then lowered her window. "I will see you when I come home from the—" A wave of surprise and pain interrupted her.

"Don't say it!" yelled Mrs. Koza, who had slid into the backseat alongside Mrs. Yee.

Mrs. Yee grinned and held her breath.

"Buckle your seat belt," Mr. Koza said over his shoulder.

"Get ready for blast off," I told Mrs. Yee.

She grinned. "Just like going to the moon. Right, Zachary?"

"Just take away the coasting."

Before Mrs. Yee could respond, Mr. Koza hit the gas. The orange car leaped away from the curb leaving me by myself in front of Coco's Cones. After a moment, I walked back into the ice cream shop where I found Coco the dog waiting for me. "There's really no such thing as coasting, is there?" I asked him.

Coco didn't speak. He didn't have to. I already knew the answer.

CHAPTER 17

A FEW MINUTES AFTER THE KOZAS DROVE away with Mrs. Yee, a young woman showed up at the ice cream shop with a couple kids in tow. "Are you open?" she asked.

"Well—" I glanced at the big, wooden pendulum clock on the wall. Besides hours, minutes, and seconds, the clock showed the month, the day, and the phases of the moon.

The woman noticed me looking at the clock. "You're not about to close, are you?"

"I—"

"Because I promised my kids that I'd get them ice cream today."

Over the last few months, I'd given a lot of thought to what kind of parent my mom had been. Now I considered the lady in front of me who was trying to keep a promise that she'd made to her own children. And then I thought of Mrs. Yee who was just about to start her own motherhood adventures. It struck me that I'd never actually considered the physical act of giving birth. Based on what I'd observed during the last few minutes, maybe it was a thrill ride that could easily lead to insanity. Maybe that's what happened to my own mom.

"Well?" said the woman. Her two children, a boy and a girl, were busy petting Coco and telling him that he was the best dog in the world.

"Just cones?" I asked.

"Cones for the kids," she told me. "I'd like a butterscotch sundae."

I stood up straight and tried to sound like I knew what I was doing. "We're out of sundaes. All we've got are cones."

"How can you be out of sundaes?"

I shot a glance at Coco. He wasn't going to teach me how to make a butterscotch sundae. "We just are, okay?"

She ended up ordering two chocolate cones, and I convinced her to try the krem z herbaty for herself. Mom and kids all left happy, which might have had something to do with the fact that I forgot to charge them.

A moment later, my father appeared on the sidewalk in front of Coco's Cones. He exchanged a few words with the mom and kids who stood outside eating their cones. Finally, he gave them a wave and stepped into the shop. "I hear you're out of sundaes," Dad said when he saw me behind the counter.

"Don't you want to know what I'm doing here?" I asked.

"The Kozas decided to go back to Poland for a few weeks, and they've left you in charge of the shop," said Dad.

"Not quite," I told him.

"Mr. and Mrs. Koza rushed to the hospital with Mrs. Yee?"

"Bingle," I said. "How did you know?"

"It's a small town, Zachary." Dad examined the tubs of ice cream in the cooler. "Any recommendations?"

Before I could answer, the door swung open again. This time it was Mr. Fines, the librarian, followed by Pammy and Skipper. "Are live dogs allowed in here?" Pammy asked.

"It's okay with me if it's okay with Coco," I said.

Pammy and Skipper turned to stare at the stuffed German shepherd.

"You know," said Mr. Fines, "I used to train dogs. I can tell from Coco's body language that he has accepted Skipper into his pack."

"Good news," Pammy said to Skipper. "You're in with the in crowd."

"Woof," said the golden mutt.

"He likes vanilla in a cone," Pammy told me.

I grabbed a scoop and filled Skipper's order. "What can I get for the rest of you?"

"Do you have any idea what you're doing?" asked Pammy.

Mr. Fines stepped behind the counter and grabbed a scoop. "Let me."

"I can put ice cream in a cone," I said.

"There are forty-seven books about ice cream at the library," he said.

"Forty-seven?"

"There's ice cream cookbooks, ice cream history books, ice cream memorabilia books, ice cream business books, and ice cream science books." Mr. Fines turned to face me. "Those are the main categories. How many ice cream books have you read?"

"None," I admitted.

"You better let me handle this." He started filling cones and passing them out.

"Don't we get to pick what we want?" Pammy asked him.

"No," Mr. Fines handed Pammy a cone filled with neon pink ice cream. Next, he gave Dad a cone filled with Coffee Break, which was coffee ice cream mixed with chocolate chips. I got a big scoop of something called Blueberry Joy.

"This is not what I would have asked for," said Dad after he tried a bite of his ice cream, "but it might be the best thing I've ever tasted."

"I wish we could hand out books this way at the library," said Mr. Fines.

"What are you all doing here?" I asked.

"Mr. Koza called city hall to ask if somebody would come over and help you lock up," Dad said.

"Why didn't he just call here?" I said.

"He was so nervous about Mrs. Yee that he dialed 911. The dispatcher transferred the call to me."

"Your dad contacted me because I know where the keys are," said Mr. Fines.

"And I was coming into the library when Mr. Fines was running out," said Pammy. "He told me what was going on, so I followed him here."

"Is there any news about Mrs. Yee?" I asked.

Mr. Fines shook his head. "Not yet."

I walked to the shop's front door and hung the CLOSED sign on the knob. "I could have locked up myself," I said.

"Not without a key." Mr. Fines reached into the ice cream cooler, lifted a tub labeled Por la Noche, and retrieved a key ring from underneath it.

"Is Por la noche Polish for key?" said Pammy.

"It's Spanish," said Mr. Fines. "It means 'for the night.'"

"As in, you need the key at night," Dad said.

"Exactly," said the librarian.

"You speak Spanish, you're a dog trainer, and you're an ice cream expert," Pammy said to Mr. Fines. "Is there anything you don't know?"

Mr. Fines shrugged. "I'm a librarian. Knowing things is my job."

I glanced at my father. "I thought that's what police officers did."

"The two jobs are not dissimilar," said Mr. Fines.

"Maybe I'll be a librarian when I grow up," said Pammy.

Mr. Fines smiled. "Who would like to try *Por la Noche*? It is regular chocolate ice cream mixed with pieces of Mexican chocolate."

Back in Copper Lake, Dad and I liked to visit the Viva Mercado, a tiny market in the center of town, to try different kinds of Mexican candy. The chocolate was dark and bitter and filled with crystal chunks of sugar and nutmeg and almonds and cinnamon. Sometimes it had little bits of chili powder in it too.

"What's Mexican chocolate?" Pammy asked.

"You might not like it," I told her. At that moment, Teddy and Rachel burst into Coco's Cones. I pointed at Rachel. "She'd definitely like it."

"Like what?" asked Rachel.

"Mrs. Yee had her baby!" announced Teddy.

Suddenly, everybody was talking at once. Mr. Fines

passed out more ice cream. Skipper started barking and running laps around the inside of the ice cream shop. Teddy tried to calm the dog down, but somehow that had the opposite effect. In all the commotion, nobody heard the door to the shop swing open.

"Excuse me?" a voice said.

I glanced toward the entrance, and my mouth dropped open.

"Excuse me?" she said again.

Slowly, the rest of the room turned to see the new person who had joined us. I took a big breath and then slowly let it out, "Hi, Mom."

CHAPTER 18

WHEN I LOOKED AT MY MOTHER, I WANTED to see a monster. I wanted to see Cruella de Vil or Bellatrix Lestrange or some kind of puppy-kicking villain from a cheesy comic book. Instead, a small, pretty, brown-haired woman stood in the doorway.

"Hi, Zachary," said Mom.

"Roberta," said Dad.

"Is that your mother?" Rachel asked me.

I nodded.

Teddy stepped forward. "Hi, Zachary's mother."

Mom gave him a nervous smile. Her hair looked darker than I remembered, and she'd cut it short. She wore a flowery blue skirt and a shirt that matched. She'd never worn anything like that in Copper Lake. It was like she was carrying a sign that said, I am not who I used to be.

"You've changed," I said out loud.

She turned to face me. "Maybe."

"Zachary didn't tell us you were so pretty," Teddy said to Mom.

She looked like she might kiss him. "You are very kind."

Mom had been in the room for less than a minute, and she was already winning people over. If I didn't do something, she'd be mayor of Falls by the end of the day.

"What are you doing here?" I asked.

Mom turned her smile on me. "What do you think I'm doing here, Zachary?"

Dad moved to my side. "Roberta," he said to Mom, "I'm sure neither Zachary nor I want to make a guess about why you do anything."

"I wanted to see you." Mom sounded hurt.

"You've seen us," I blurted out. "Now you can go."

Pammy, Rachel, and Teddy shuffled uncomfortably. Even Skipper hid beneath a table. Mr. Fines stepped out from behind the counter. "I hate to interrupt," he said, "but I have to get back to the library."

"Thank you for the key," I told him.

"You're welcome." Just before Mr. Fines left the shop, he stopped at the door to give Coco a quick pat on the head. "Keep an eye on things," the librarian whispered to the dog.

"Can I get an ice cream cone?" Mom asked.

Dad shifted his weight from one foot to the other. He seemed to be struggling with some decision. After a moment, he lifted his head and spoke to Mom. "They're all out of cones."

Teddy looked down at the huge rainbow colored cone in his hand then hid it behind his back.

"I see," Mom said. She turned her attention my way. "Have you missed me, Zachary?"

Suddenly, my mouth was as dry as sawdust. I said nothing.

"Have you missed me a little?" she asked.

Still nothing.

Mom bit her lower lip. "Are you at least happy to see me?"

"I don't know," I choked out.

Mom looked a little stunned.

"Zachary," she said, "I know I did not make the most gracious exit, but you have to understand. Your father—"

"Stop," I said.

"Let me explain."

I shook my head. "I want you to go."

"But I just got here."

Dad stepped to my side.

"I want you to go," I said again.

"Right now?"

I nodded.

Mom stood a little straighter, but then she seemed to crumple a little bit. "Do you mean forever?" she asked me.

Before I could speak, Teddy interrupted.

"No!"

"Teddy," said Rachel, "this is not about us."

"No," Teddy said again. "Forever is too much." I watched my friend reach out and take my mother's hand. Then he took my hand too. "One day," he said to me, "you'll really, really want to talk to your Mom." He turned to face his sister. "Tell Zachary that forever is too long."

Rachel bit her lip. "It's a long time," she finally said.

"He doesn't want you to go away forever," Teddy said to my mother.

Mom glanced between me and Teddy. "That's good."

I pulled my hand away from Teddy's. "But I don't want to see her yet." I looked straight at my mother. "I don't want to see you today."

Teddy put his hands in his pockets and backed away. Mom placed her own hands on her hips. Suddenly, she looked very angry. "I've come a long way. I've been driving since yesterday. I'm here now, and—"

"You can't come and go as you please!" I shouted.

Mom's head snapped back as if I'd slapped her in the face. She turned to Dad for help.

"The boy's right," said Dad.

I watched my mother take a step backward. It was as if she were shrinking right there in front of me. "But you asked me to come," she said.

"I shouldn't have had to ask," said Dad. "You should have come sooner."

Mom turned to me. "Zachary," she said, "I'm sorry, but—"

Rachel stepped forward as if she were my own personal bodyguard. "We don't want to hear it."

"Actually," said Dad, "I think we do want to hear it."

"Oh." Rachel stepped back. "Don't mind me."

I reached out and took Rachel's hand. "Thanks," I whispered to her.

"We loved you," Dad said to Mom. "We still love you. But you blew it. You hurt me, and you hurt my son."

"He's my son too," Mom said in a small voice.

"You haven't acted like it lately," Dad said.

Mom didn't reply.

"Being in a family is like being on a roller coaster ride," Dad continued. "I get that. There's good times and bad times." He stared at Mom square in the face. "But you got off the ride."

"What if I want to get back on?"

I wanted to shout again, but I spoke in as even a voice as possible. "That's not up to you."

Rachel let go of my hand. She turned and marched behind the counter where she grabbed a sugar cone and a metal scoop. She stuffed the cone full of *krem z herbaty* and then shoved it toward my mother. "Here."

"What's this?" said Mom.

"Take it," said Rachel.

Mom didn't respond.

"You wanted ice cream," Rachel said.

Mom reached out and accepted the cone. A bit of *krem z herbaty* dripped onto her wrist. Without thinking, she lifted her hand and licked the ice cream off her skin. Her face lit up. "That's good."

"I know," I said.

"Thank you for the ice cream," said Mom.

"Good-bye," I told her.

"For now?" she asked.

Rachel came over and stood next to me.

"Okay," I said.

Dad crossed the floor and pushed the shop door open. "Roberta," he said, "I'll walk you to your car."

Mom took another lick from her cone. She gave me a sad smile. "Can I call you on the phone?" she asked.

"Yes," said Teddy. "You should call him."

Mom looked at me.

"Okay," I said again.

Mom turned to leave, and I watched her walk away. I came out from behind the counter to watch her walk away. When Dad pulled the door open, Skipper hopped to his feet, sprinted past my parents, then shot out to the curb. He stopped beside a little red Volkswagen with Colorado license plates. It was Mom's car. The dog lifted a leg and peed on her back bumper. At the same time, I felt a warm hand slip into mine. It was Rachel. "I knew I liked that dog," she said.

I didn't say anything. If I did, I might have burst into tears. My mother was driving away again. This time, it was my fault.

CHAPTER 19

ON THE LAST SATURDAY IN AUGUST, with school just a few days away, Teddy, Rachel, Pammy, and I worked to put the final touches on Tilley's Park. News about the project had spread around Falls, so we weren't alone anymore. Mayor Zimmerman promised that the pond would be available for winter skating if the place could be in good shape by Labor Day, so a few more volunteers seemed to show up every afternoon. I saw Coach Behr, a few football players, and even Mrs. Yee had arrived with her new baby, her husband, and most of the band.

I'd heard from Mom a couple times since the day Mrs. Yee's baby was born. Once she phoned from a ship sailing somewhere off the coast of Canada. Another time, she let us know that she'd be stuck for two days in New York City. Dad and I found a bus that ran between Falls and New York, so we met her for lunch in a park near the Empire State Building. That was pretty amazing. My mother let us know that she'd been promoted to something called "Shore Excursion Manager" on the cruise ship where she worked, and she'd be heading to Australia and New Zealand soon. "When you get older," she told me, "I could help you get a summer job aboard ship."

"We'll see," I said.

In the meantime, I focused on working at the park and pretending that summer would never end.

"Summer always feels like it will last forever," said Pammy, who knelt beside her dad and yanked weeds from beneath the skating pavilion.

Rachel leaned on a rake. "The whole thing goes by in a flash."

"I like how crickets and toads sing all night long during summer," said Teddy.

"Long days and warm nights, they make everything come alive," said Mrs. Robertson, who'd just finished planting a row of chrysanthemums around the edge of the pavilion.

"And now it's almost gone," said Rachel.

Mrs. Robertson turned and faced Rachel. "Honey," she said, "you are bumming me out. Go take a walk or something."

"I'm just saying—" Rachel began.

"You go with her," the Queen of Everything ordered me. "Protect her from squirrels."

"Squirrels," said Teddy. "I better come, too."

Rachel gave me a quick smile, then turned to her

brother. "I think Zachary and I can handle it without you this time."

"You stay here," Mrs. Robertson told him. "I want to talk to you about a job."

"What job?" he asked.

"It's a volunteer position to start, but it could lead to bigger things. You'll be special assistant to the city parks manager."

"Who is the city parks manager?" Teddy asked.

Mayor Zimmerman pointed at Mrs. Robertson. "You're looking at her."

Rachel and I took the opportunity to slip away. Together, we walked along the edge of the pond, then turned to follow a path leading up a steep bank into the woods.

"Where are we going?" I asked.

"Follow me," said Rachel. "I've been meaning to show you something."

We passed a few fat boulders and several stands of scraggly maples. I could hear a thousand birds around us, but I couldn't see a single one. We finally stopped beside a pile of rough stones that looked like it might have been a wall once. "What's this?" I asked.

"It's a house," said Rachel.

I prodded one of the stones with my toe. "It doesn't look like a house."

"It's what's left of the Tilley's house," said Rachel.

"As in Tilley's park?" I asked.

"They're the ones that gave the park to the town." Rachel pointed at the thick woods spread all around us. "They used to own all this about a hundred years ago."

"Wow."

"I bet you would do something like that, Zachary."

I sat on the pile of rocks. "Like what?"

"Give it all away." Rachel sat too. She didn't speak for a long time. Finally, she said, "I couldn't let go of a single pebble."

"Why not?"

She picked up a stone. "What if I needed it for something?"

"Like what?" I asked.

"I don't know," said Rachel. "I like to be ready for anything."

"Instead of hoarding all your stones," I said, "you could just ask for help sometimes."

She stared at the remains of the rock wall, which snaked away through the trees. It made the outline of a foundation. "Maybe I'm asking for help right now."

And that's when I kissed her.

I just leaned in close and did it. I put my lips on hers, and she did not pull away, and she did not punch me in the face. And I'd like to say that I saw fireworks and that the planets stopped in their orbits and that the squirrels in the trees around us stopped to whistle and cheer, but if any of that happened, I didn't notice. I did notice that when I smiled, I liked the feeling of Rachel's mouth smiling back. After a little while, we leaned apart. Rachel turned toward me, a big smile spread across her face. "Can I tell you something?" she said.

"What is it?" I wondered if she was going to tell me that I was a very good kisser.

"It's not about the kissing," Rachel said as if she could read my mind.

"Then what is it?" I admit I was a little disappointed.

"You are a good friend."

"Is this how you treat all your friends?" I asked.

"No." Rachel leaned forward as if she might kiss me again, but then she stopped. "Listen."

"What?" I asked.

"Don't you hear it?"

I shook my head, still too dazed from the kiss to speak in full sentences.

"A trumpet," she said.

And then I heard the sound. A single, sweet note rising through the trees. It was soft and growing from below.

"Is that Teddy?" I asked.

"I don't think so."

She was right. Teddy was good, but even in one note I could hear something clean and powerful that Teddy did not have yet. I stood. "That's my Dad."

Rachel got to her feet and took my hand. "Come on!"

Without waiting, she started to race down the hill and back toward the pond. We ran through the woods and soon we were off the path, leaping over dead logs and bouncing off small saplings. We tumbled out of the trees, and it was all I could do to stop myself from hurtling into the pond. My father, a couple hundred feet away, did not notice us arrive. He stayed focused on the horn and continued to play.

"Look," Rachel said breathlessly. She pointed toward the pavilion at the opposite end of the water. The porch was covered with friends and volunteers. All around, people had stopped their sweeping and painting and cleaning. Work had come to a halt so that everybody could listen to my father. Music floated and echoed around us and through the park. It was the tune Dad had started for me in the desert back in Copper Lake.

"This must be your song," Rachel said.

"How do you know about that?"

"Teddy can't keep a secret," she reminded me.

Rachel and I stood close together and listened. And even though they could not see us, we were surrounded by friends. Near the pavilion, the Kozas were scooping ice cream out of a cooler. Mr. Fines stood clapping in time to the music. Teddy sat in the grass between Mrs. Robertson and his dad. In the meantime, Skipper, who'd just spotted a couple fat geese, tore through the crowd and turned into a golden blur of a dog.

I turned to Rachel and noticed a thin scratch across her cheek. It must have happened during our mad dash down the hill. I touched her face. "Are you okay?"

She nodded. "Yes. Are you?"

I didn't answer. I didn't have the right words. I didn't have enough words. Instead, I took her hand. We would join the crowd in a little while, but first I led Rachel into the shade of a tree where no one could see us. We sat against the rough trunk while music filled the air. I recognized the tune from the first time I'd heard it. All the original ingredients were still there, the coyotes and the stars and the sadness from the desert. But now there was more. There were green trees, and good friends, and a town built on rolling hills. There were even reggae snippets and pieces of tunes I'd played with Teddy this summer. And through it all, I could hear a hopeful sound. The minor chords had not gone away, but they were no longer the main part of this song.

"Zachary in B-flat," said Rachel. "I like it a lot."

"Me too."

I imagined notes hanging in the sky like fireflies or Christmas lights. And we sat without speaking while summer came to an end, and the moment and the music wrapped like arms around us.

ACKNOWLEDGMENTS

Thank you to editor, instigator, collaborator, co-creator, and great friend Nancy Mercado, whose gigantic leaps of faith in me are stunning and sometimes frightening. Thanks also to all the fantastic people at Roaring Brook Press. I am very excited to be a member of the RB family.

I rely on the extraordinary community of children's book writers and illustrators whose work astounds, teaches, and inspires me: Laurie Halse Anderson, Kate DiCamillo, Deborah Heiligman, David Lubar, Lauren Tarshis, Deborah Wiles, Nancy Werlin, all my SCBWI friends, and many, many more. Closer to home, Mark Harris, Joyce Hinnefeld, Ruth Knaffo Setton, and Virginia Wiles are fabulous friends and amazing writers who keep me focused and moving forward on many fronts . . . Thank you!

My remarkable coworkers at Northampton Community College put up with me Monday through Friday and sometimes beyond. NCC is a place filled with people who believe that being excellent is worth the extra effort. I am very proud to be a part of it. I am deeply indebted (sometimes literally) to booksellers and librarians everywhere. Special thanks to Jane Clugston at the Moravian Bookshop in Bethlehem, PA; Jennifer Cogan O'Leary at the Bucks County Free Library; Janet Fricker at the Bethlehem Area Public Library; Ellen Majer at Booktenders Secret Garden in

Doylestown, PA; Doug Mohr at Lion Around Books in Quakertown, PA; and many others as well.

My parents, Salvatore and Maureen; my sister, Michelle, my grandparents; and an army of aunts, uncles, cousins, and lifelong friends raised me to believe that a good story is always worth the time it takes to tell it. I deeply appreciate their many, many gifts, which include great joy, deep faith, fierce love, fantastic food, family history, and good timing. Speaking of faith, nobody ever made a bigger leap than my wife, Debbie, when she accepted my proposal of marriage. Her love, joy, patience, and encouragement sustain me. The same is true for my children, Nicholas and Gabrielle, who laugh at my dumb jokes, defeat me in endless board games, and simply make me happy every single day.

Finally, my heartfelt appreciation goes to the kind and generous readers who spend time with my work. Your imagination brings these stories to life. Thank you.

Go Fish!

GOFISH

PAUL ACAMPORA

© Adam Atkinson

What did you want to be when you grew up?
I planned to be an astronaut, a veterinarian, a fighter pilot, an engineer, a musician, a farmer, a florist, a travel agent, a truck driver, or a gardener.

What's your most embarrassing childhood memory?
When I was five years old, I accidentally cut off my sister's ear. I really did feel bad about it. (But not as bad as my sister!)

What's your favorite childhood memory?
I can't pick just one. Here's a few that I still think about: playing the piano with my grandfather . . . building a soapbox derby car with my dad . . . Saturday morning tag sales with my mom . . . summer days on Rhode Island beaches . . . bodysurfing gigantic waves after a storm . . . autumn leaves piled higher than my head . . . riding a pony named Misty in the Mum Festival Parade . . . my sister and I eating ice cream cones at the Naugatuck Valley Mall . . . listening to aunts and uncles tell stories over long, slow meals . . . wandering around the library after school . . . sneaking my dog

into my bed . . . sipping a Coke on my grandparents' back porch . . . I've got lots more where those came from. I am very lucky that way.

As a young person, who did you look up to most?

When I was young, my grandfathers seemed about as different as two people could be. One was strong and stern and quiet. The other was funny and musical, and he liked to sleep till noon. One grandfather worked in a factory his whole life. The other owned a music shop with his brother. One had a quick smile and a thick Italian accent. The other was a remarkable horseman, a great storyteller, an easy artist, and a heck of a poker player. I wanted to be like both of them. I still do.

What was your favorite thing about school?

My favorite thing about school was my friends. I don't mean that I didn't like math, science, history, and the rest. I liked all that a lot. I was a pretty good student too, but friends are always the best.

What was your least favorite thing about school?

The color green. I went to a Catholic school and had to wear a uniform—green pants, white shirt, and a green tie—every single day. It wasn't pretty.

What were your hobbies as a kid? What are your hobbies now?

As a kid, I enjoyed playing the piano. I collected coins with my grandfather. My father and I rebuilt an old sports car. Today, I enjoy kayaking with my wife and kids. I love going to the movies. I'm learning how to play the ukulele. I still have the coin collection. It's fun to sift through it and imagine where the old dimes and nickels and pennies might have been before they got to me.

What was your first job, and what was your "worst" job?

I've had a lot of jobs. For my first job, I cut my neighbors' lawns. Then I delivered newspapers for the Bristol Press in Bristol, Connecticut. Some of my jobs have required some pretty dirty work—cleaning out elevator shafts, collecting dirty dishes off a cafeteria conveyor belt, scrubbing middle-school toilets, spraying chemicals onto thousands of tiny, plastic parts—but those jobs have rarely been terrible. The worst jobs are the ones that force you to spend time with sour, petty, unkind people. There's not enough money in the world to make those situations worthwhile.

What book is on your nightstand now?

I've always got several books going at once. Right now, I'm in the middle of *By the Great Horn Spoon* by Sid Fleischman; *The River of Doubt: Theodore Roosevelt's Darkest Journey* by Candice Millard; *City of Orphans* by Avi; *Space Chronicles: Facing the Ultimate Frontier* by Neil deGrasse Tyson; *True Grit* by Charles Portis; *Guy Langman, Crime Scene Procrastinator* by Josh Berk; *I'll Be There* by Holly Goldberg Sloan; *Please Ignore Vera Dietz* by A.S. King; *The Mismeasure of Man* by Stephen Jay Gould; *Bird by Bird* by Anne Lamott.

How did you celebrate publishing your first book?

I have a day job, and I had to go to work on the publication day of my first book. When I got home, my family surprised me with cake and ice cream and a big sign on the front of the house which said FAMOUS AUTHOR LIVES HERE! That was awesome.

Where do you write your books?

My schedule is pretty hectic. I try to carve regular writing times into my calendar, but it rarely works. As a result, I write on legal pads and computers and scratch paper wherever and whenever I have a few free minutes. That can happen at my desk during a lunch break, at the kitchen table before everybody's awake, in waiting rooms while my kids dance or act or take music lessons. . . . I really write just about anywhere.

What sparked your imagination for *Rachel Spinelli Punched Me in the Face*?

I was at a local park, and I overheard a small girl hollering at a group of teenage boys. She was scolding them for teasing her brother. She was just so confident and brave. The boys were laughing at her because she was very small, but they also obeyed. I started wondering what if . . . what if . . . what if. . . . From there, the character of Rachel just jumped to life.

Have you ever lived in a town like Falls?

Falls has a lot in common with Bristol, Connecticut, where I grew up. I also drew a bunch from Quakertown and the surrounding towns in Pennsylvania. There are also dashes from Colorado towns—especially Basalt and Snowmass—where people have been very kind to me.

Do you play any musical instruments?

I play the piano badly and the ukulele even worse than that.

What was your childhood best friend like?

My best friends are generally strong-willed, honest, opinionated, loyal, very busy, very smart, and they love to laugh. In short, they are a lot like Rachel Spinelli.

What would your superhero name be?

Pelo Azul.

What would you order at Rachel's family's diner?
French fries and a strawberry milkshake.

What challenges do you face in the writing process, and how do you overcome them?
Finding regular time to write is a big challenge. Rather than wait for a block of time, I'm sort of writing all the time. I constantly jot down ideas, lines of dialogue, and character descriptions in note-books and on scraps of paper that I carry everywhere I go. That way, when I get 15 minutes or an hour to write, I can come to the work with some ingredients.

What makes you laugh out loud?
Anything and everything. It is not unusual for me to laugh at inappropriate times.

What do you do on a rainy day?
Read, write, play board games, wrestle with dogs, eat ice cream, repeat.

What's your idea of fun?
Read, write, play board games, wrestle with dogs, eat ice cream, repeat.

If you were stranded on a desert island, who would you want for company?
Debbie Acampora (my wife).

If you could travel in time, where would you go and what would you do?
I would go to Washington, D.C., during the Civil War in hopes that I could join President Lincoln and his friends for a casual evening of

conversation and storytelling. Abraham Lincoln was renowned for his laughter, joke-telling, and great stories.

What's the best advice you have ever received about writing?
Pretend you know what you're doing and just keep going.

What advice do you wish someone had given you when you were younger?
Pretend you know what you're doing and just keep going.

Do you ever get writer's block? What do you do to get back on track?
Writer's block hasn't been a problem for me. If I'm feeling stuck—which is different than writer's block—I might turn my attention to a different activity for awhile and then come back to my story later. Sometimes, I just go ahead and write really, really badly. Fixing bad writing is generally about the same amount of work as writing well (which I never do in my first drafts anyway).

What do you want readers to remember about your books?
E.B. White said: "All that I hope to say in books, all that I ever hope to say, is that I love the world." That sums it up nicely.

What should people know about you?
I am very lucky. I am always winning raffles and cakewalks and door prizes and Bingo. I am not one of those people who says, "I never win anything."

What do you like best about yourself?
I am not one of those people who says, "I never win anything."

**Do you have any strange or funny habits?
Did you when you were a kid?**
I talk to myself—out loud and in my head—with great enthusiasm.

Embark on new adventures
with these exciting SQUARE FISH titles

**The Girl Who
Circumnavigated
Fairyland**
Catherynne M. Valente
Illustrations by Ana Juan
ISBN 978-1-250-01019-3

Time Cat
Lloyd Alexander
ISBN 978-0-312-63213-7

The Little Secret
Kate Saunders
ISBN 978-0-312-67427-4

The Kneebone Boy
Ellen Potter
ISBN 978-0-312-67432-8

A Wrinkle in Time
Madeleine L'Engle
ISBN 978-1-250-00467-3

**The Secret
of Zoom**
Lynne Jonell
ISBN 978-0-312-65933-2

READ ALL FOUR JOEY PIGZA BOOKS!
AVAILABLE FROM SQUARE FISH

Joey Pigza Swallowed the Key
978-0-312-62355-5 • $6.99 US / $7.99 Can

Joey Pigza's "dud meds" are not controlling his wild mood swings like they're supposed to. Is he going to end up stuck in the special-ed program?

National Book Award Finalist!

Joey Pigza Loses Control
978-0-312-66101-4 • $6.99 US / $7.99 Can

Joey Pigza finally has his behavior under control when he visits his dad for the first time in years. But can he keep it that way when his dad cuts off his meds?

Newbery Honor Book!

I Am Not Joey Pigza
978-0-312-66100-7 • $6.99 US / $7.99 Can

When Joey's deadbeat dad wins the lottery, he wants to change everything about the Pigza family. But if he does, how will Joey know who he really is?

What Would Joey Pigza Do?
978-0-312-66102-1 • $6.99 US / $7.99 Can

Joey tries to make friends with the meanest girl he knows, while his long-separated parents suddenly start fighting—or are they flirting?

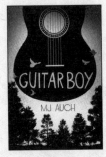

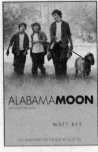
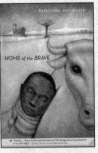